"There are a l[...] in love with th[...]

Maribeth turned to face him. "It's terrible when you think someone loves you, and when you love them, and then—" she blinked, and her tears fell free "—you find out that they don't."

Ryan looked directly at her now, and she knew he undoubtedly saw the pain in her eyes. He'd opened up to her, and she could feel herself wanting to do the same.

But what would happen if she did? What if the two of them did become close, and then the truth of her past came out?

"You've felt that before, too, haven't you?" he asked. "You thought someone loved you, really believed that they cared about you, and then you found out that they didn't."

She couldn't deny it, so she nodded. "And the worst part is, once you've been treated so badly, it's difficult to open your heart again, isn't it?"

She hadn't intended to, but she'd moved a little closer as she spoke.

Books by Renee Andrews

Love Inspired

Her Valentine Family
Healing Autumn's Heart
Picture Perfect Family
Love Reunited
Heart of a Rancher
Bride Wanted
Yuletide Twins
Mommy Wanted
Small-Town Billionaire

RENEE ANDREWS

spends a lot of time in the gym. No, she isn't working out. Her husband, a former All-American gymnast, co-owns ACE Cheer Company, an all-star cheerleading company. She is thankful the talented kids at the gym don't have a problem when she brings her laptop and writes while they sweat. When she isn't writing, she's typically traveling with her husband, bragging about their two sons and daughter-in-law or spoiling their grandsons.

Renee is a kidney donor and actively supports organ donation. In 2013, Renee, her husband, J.R., and their oldest son, Rene, competed as team Hello Kidney on the American Bible Challenge to raise money for living donors and to raise awareness for the need for living donors. If you are considering becoming a living donor, ask her about how you can also save a life by sharing your spare! Or check out the "living donor" section of her website. She welcomes prayer requests and loves to hear from readers. Write to her at Renee@ReneeAndrews.com or visit her website at www.reneeandrews.com. You can find her on Facebook as AuthorReneeAndrews, or follow @ReneeAndrews on Twitter.

Small-Town Billionaire

Renee Andrews

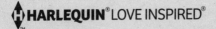

Recycling programs
for this product may
not exist in your area.

 LOVE INSPIRED BOOKS

ISBN-13: 978-0-373-87909-0

SMALL-TOWN BILLIONAIRE

Copyright © 2014 by Renee Andrews

www.Harlequin.com

Printed in U.S.A.

There is nothing concealed that will not be
disclosed, or hidden that will not be made known.
—*Luke* 12:2

For Matt McCallum, the young man I met four years ago and gave a kidney to that same year— what an awesome opportunity to see God work that miracle! And for Brittany McCallum, Matt's beautiful wife and baby Ryan's mommy. And finally for Ryan Zeringue McCallum, the precious little angel who has stolen all our hearts. I hope your first birthday is as special as you!

KK loves you all…big as the sky!

Chapter One

"Uncle Ryan, are you gonna watch me help the kids at the church camp today? I get to do all the activities and stuff with them, but I'm an instructor, too. See?" Abi, Landon and Georgiana Cutter's eight-year-old daughter, pointed to the sheriff's badge on her pink T-shirt. Sure enough, Instructor was printed across the middle.

Ryan Brooks still couldn't get used to the whole uncle thing. Technically, he wasn't her uncle. Landon was John Cutter's brother, and Ryan's sister Dana was married to John. That definitely made Dana Abi's aunt, but how Ryan got roped into this uncle business was beyond him. However, things worked differently in the South than in his Chicago world, and since the church camp occurred on his sister's ranch, where he was stuck for the time being, he might as well get used to "Uncle Ryan."

"I do see," he said. "What exactly are you instructing them to do?"

Her pigtails bobbed as she shook her head and gave him a little eye roll, strawberry lashes hitting her brows with the maneuver. "Riding, silly. How to put the saddle on, and why to wear a helmet and how to be safe." She glanced at Ryan's cast-bound leg. "And how not to fall off."

"Thaaanks," he said. The cast, or rather, the blown knee in it, was the entire reason he remained in Alabama instead of returning to Chicago and Brooks International. He'd let Dana talk him into running his business remotely while he went through rehab here for what the doctors called the unhappy triad: a torn ACL, PCL and medial meniscus. Or, in layman's terms, a blown left knee.

If Ryan didn't know any better, though, he'd say his sister was glad her new black stallion had tossed Ryan two weeks ago and equally glad that his therapy would take another month.

Abi, missing the sarcasm, sent a spray of freckles dancing with her smile. "You're welcome!" She'd spent the past fifteen minutes gathering red and pink azalea blooms from the bushes that lined John and Dana's porch, and she now clutched the bright blossoms in her hand like a wedding bouquet.

"I'm sure your mama will like those flowers," Ryan said.

"Oh, I took Mama and Aunt Dana some already. These are for Miss Maribeth. She's at the barn with Aunt Dana."

Maribeth. The unique name sparked the memory of the equally unique woman. He'd only met her once, with a brief introduction at John and Dana's wedding, but he remembered her vividly. Dark brown, nearly black hair reaching her waist. Olive skin and exotic eyes. A full mouth. *Stunning.* The word invaded his thoughts and remained there.

"You going back inside to work?" Abi asked, pulling his thoughts from the memory and reminding Ryan that the majority of his time since his injury had been spent either at rehab or in John and Dana's cabin. He was so ready to get back to living again, back to Chicago. But first he wanted to see if his memory had embellished the beauty of the woman with the unique name.

"No, I think I'll go out to the barn," he said.

"You want to go with me?" she asked, and Ryan noticed her frown slightly at the crutches propped against the porch railing.

"No, it'll take me a little while. You go on ahead."

"Okay," she said, unable to hide her excitement as she darted away.

Maneuvering on crutches from the house to the barn wasn't easy; the soft earth gave with every step, and Ryan had to concentrate more on his pace than on his goal. Halfway there, he met Abi, running from the barn toward her house, the other large log cabin on the Cutter ranch.

"Miss Maribeth loved the flowers!" she yelled, and continued her sprint without waiting for a response from Ryan.

He continued his trek toward the barn and wondered if it was actually as hot outside as it seemed. True, the first week of June would be naturally warm, but he attributed the heat he experienced to the workout from using the crutches in the soft farm dirt. Sweat beads pushed free from his temples the way they normally did when he worked out in the gym. And he was barely moving.

For a moment, he considered turning around, heading back to John and Dana's cabin and forgoing this bizarre curiosity toward his sister's friend. But then he got close enough to see around the barn's edge, and the vision nearly stopped him in his tracks.

Maribeth Walton stood beside Dana holding Abi's bouquet of flowers. Her inky hair caught the sun and shone brilliantly as it billowed against her back. Ryan would be lying if he said his interest hadn't gotten the best of him when Dana mentioned that Maribeth would be one of the counselors for the church youth retreats at the ranch this month. Their chance encounter at John and Dana's wedding had haunted him ever since. She'd appeared immune to the typical effect Ryan had on women, a fact that both irritated and intrigued him.

Unfortunately, he'd had the feeling once before, the first time he saw Nannette Kelly. Ryan set his jaw and reminded himself how *that* had turned out. But in spite of the memory of how his last infatuation—okay, love—had ended, he couldn't stop his progress toward the barn. Dana had already looked his way, and her visitor followed suit. Couldn't very well turn around and hobble back to the house now.

Hobble. How embarrassing. If he were a normal guy, Maribeth Walton wouldn't look at him twice, with his cast-covered leg and unshaven face. He couldn't recall whether he'd combed his hair.

But he wasn't a normal guy. In his world, how he looked or acted didn't matter. Nannette had shown him that females weren't interested in him; they only wanted what he could give them. Money. Power. The Brooks name.

Ryan shouldn't be concerned about whether or

not he impressed Maribeth Walton. But even so, he couldn't take his eyes away from her as he neared the two women.

Today her hair fell freely, wildly, and she pushed the dark locks from her face as she tossed her head back and laughed at something Dana said. At the wedding, that thick mane had been braided and contained, a yellow satin ribbon woven within the dark locks. Ryan wasn't certain why he remembered the fact about the ribbon, particularly the color. He never paid attention to details. Those items didn't matter in the entire scheme of things.

"Note what's important—flush everything else. Don't waste precious brain cells on the negligible." One of his father's more notable spoutings of wisdom and typically a rule Ryan lived by.

So why did he remember her hair, or the ribbon? Or the fact that she'd smelled like cinnamon and apples? Or that she'd been dressed as if she was ready for a Parisian runway? She'd worn a flowing bright blue dress with silver accents and stylish, crazy high heels. Sure, everyone in town had dressed up for the occasion, but there was something different about Maribeth that set her apart from the rest. And at the reception, in spite of his past history with Nannette, Ryan had sought the lady out for conversation.

She'd coolly said hello and then left him to talk to someone else.

Today, in a bright yellow blouse, hot pink skirt and snazzy boots, she again stood out from the rural surroundings. Maribeth, this country girl in north Alabama, happened to be the only woman since Nannette who had caught his interest for more than a passing glance…and the only one who didn't care whether he looked her way or not.

"Hey, Ryan, how was your rehab this morning?" Dana asked as soon as he was within earshot.

"It went okay," he said. John had taken Ryan to his therapy sessions since Dana's morning sickness got the best of her again. In her third month of pregnancy, she still had a tough go several mornings a week and hadn't ventured out of her bedroom before John and Ryan had left. Ryan hated being dependent on them to drive him around, but there was no way he could drive in this cast.

Then again, back in Chicago he had a driver to take him where he needed to go. But this felt different, having to rely on his family to help him out. He didn't mind paying employees for the task, but having people simply help him out of the goodness of their hearts wasn't something he was used to. Or something he wanted to get used to. He needed to leave Alabama. The sooner the better.

"You've met Maribeth, haven't you?" Dana continued, tilting her head toward the petite woman who looked even prettier close up.

Almond-shaped chocolate eyes locked with his, and a light breeze carried that scent of apples and cinnamon he remembered. She quickly glanced toward the horses grazing nearby. Normally when people met the CEO of Brooks International, they treated him with the same regard Ryan's father had always received when he led the *Fortune* 500 company. They stared or gawked or whipped out a phone and snapped a picture. The paparazzi typically followed Ryan around to snag photos of him at events, so he was used to the natural response.

But he wasn't used to this.

He cleared his throat. "Yes, we met at your wedding," he answered, giving his voice the tone he carried at a press conference or board meeting. One of power and authority. Confidence.

"Your speech will let them know you are in control. Always maintain control," Lawrence Brooks would say.

But Ryan's control slipped a fraction when the gorgeous lady turned her attention back to him, tilted her head and asked, "We met?"

Maribeth saw the flash in the rich guy's eyes when she didn't acknowledge their first encounter at the wedding. And when Dana's laughter filled the air, she had to bite her inner cheek to keep from laughing, too. Undoubtedly, Ryan Brooks felt he was worth remembering. She knew the type, despised the type, and was ready for this conversation to be over so she could prepare to welcome the kids to camp.

"Wow, Ryan, you must have really made an impression," Dana said, attempting to smother her giggles with her hand.

"Obviously." He studied Maribeth as if she'd sprouted another head, and again, she looked away. Easier than staring at the beautiful male and giving away the fact that he made her knees a bit weak. It bothered her more than she cared to admit that she noticed the way his beard shadow highlighted the strong line of his jaw, or how his sandy hair complimented the blue in his eyes, like sand meeting the sea. Or that he was taller than she remembered, several inches taller. And that his shoulders were broader than she recalled.

Had she really noticed all of that in her brief glance?

She swallowed. Who was she kidding? Practically every woman in the U.S. had seen the magazine covers featuring America's most eligible bachelor billionaire. He was a modern JFK Jr., with the looks and the money that went along with the title, exactly the kind of guy Maribeth would have given everything to—had given everything to—seven years ago.

Not again. Never again.

She'd moved to Claremont to get away from the possibility of falling for another guy like Ryan Brooks. What were the chances of running into a wealthy man who'd sweep her off her feet and smash her heart in this tiny town?

Pretty good, when you considered the fact that Dana Brooks had become Dana Cutter and had also become one of Maribeth's dearest friends. Naturally, her brother would visit.

But that didn't mean Maribeth had to be overly friendly to the guy.

As it was, though, she wasn't even being nice. Not very Christian, in the whole scheme of things.

Help me, God. This is my weakness, guys like him, and for some reason, You're putting me face-to-face with it, with him. And Ryan Brooks? He'd be number one on the list of way too handsome and way too rich for his own good. Definitely for my own good. Are you trying to teach me to be strong, Lord?

Maribeth remembered the Bible verse from First Corinthians that Brother Henry had discussed in yesterday's sermon. The one that said God will not let you be tempted more than you can bear.

Okay, God. I can be nice.

She forced a tiny smile. "I think I do remember

meeting you at the wedding." When she saw the curve of a grin tease the edge of his beautiful mouth, she added, "I believe you wore a navy suit." Maribeth knew for certain that he'd worn a gray Brioni Vanquish valued at the same price as a modest Claremont home. She actually had a photo of Ryan Brooks wearing a similar suit on the wall at her store, and she chastised herself for the lie. She'd just promised God she'd be nice!

Forgive me, Lord.

What made her want to goad this guy?

Any impression of a smile disappeared. "I don't think so," he said, studying her as though he knew she remembered the exact color of suit he wore to the event. And the fact that it fit him perfectly, the same way she tried to fit her customers when they visited her consignment store.

"Oh, Maribeth," Dana said, still smiling from her laugh, "his suit was gray. I asked Ryan to wear gray, since that's what color John and Landon wore. Remember? You helped me pick out all of the colors for the wedding."

Maribeth nodded. "Yes, that's right. I do remember now." She picked at a loose string at the end of her sleeve to keep from looking at the guy. Then she heard the blessed sound of crunching gravel and turned her attention to the driveway, where an older-model silver BMW made its way toward the barn. "Oh, there's Jessica Martin. She said she'd be bringing Nathan and Lainey a little early. I'll go make sure all of their paperwork is done." She turned and started walking away from Dana and her way-too-attractive brother.

"Good to see you again, Maribeth."

She could keep walking and pretend she didn't hear

him, but she was less than six feet away. So she pivoted, forced another smile and then, unfortunately, emitted another lie. "You, too."

Please, God, forgive me again. And if it be Your will, send him back to his home...and away from mine.

By Thursday, Maribeth had successfully avoided any additional contact with Ryan Brooks, aka her ultimate temptation and undeniable reminder of her biggest mistake. The feat wasn't that difficult, thanks to his rehab sessions in the morning and her quick departure from the ranch every afternoon to run her store on the square. For the most part, she hardly remembered he was in town.

She paired a woven bracelet with an orange sundress and sandals similar to the outfit Hayden Panettiere had worn to a premiere last month and wondered whether Ryan had attended the same premiere. Then she shook her head and silently chastised herself for allowing the gorgeous man to invade her thoughts again. And to make matters worse, her customers seemed equally intrigued with the good-looking rich guy.

"Oh, wow. Look, Nadia. There he is." Jasmine Waddell, a nineteen-year-old blonde beauty, pointed to one of the photos on Maribeth's celebrity fashion wall. "Can you believe he's here? In Claremont?" she continued, and Maribeth knew before looking that her finger had landed on a photo of Ryan. Since Consigning Women focused on ladies' clothes, most of the photos were of women; however, Maribeth often used pictures from red carpet galas, and naturally, several of the women had a nice-looking man at their side. Ryan

Brooks happened to be that guy in no fewer than three of her displayed photos.

"I've seen those pictures before," Nadia Berry said. "But I've seen him in person at the Cutters' ranch."

Jasmine's blond hair formed a silky cape as she jerked around to face Nadia. Her blue eyes bristled with excitement. "Shut up. You saw him? I've been looking all over town just hoping to get a glimpse, and you've actually seen him? I knew I should've signed up to help with that camp. Is it too late to volunteer, Maribeth?"

Maribeth swallowed. She could use the help, especially since two more kids were joining the group tomorrow, but there were only two days left in this week's camp, and her own past experience kept her from wanting to put Jasmine anywhere near Ryan. "I believe we've got this week handled," she said.

But when Jasmine's face fell, Maribeth added, "You can volunteer for next week, if you want." She couldn't turn down a teen's offer to volunteer at a church camp, especially when she could use her assistance next week. "However, I'm not certain you would see Ryan Brooks that much. He goes to the hospital for his rehab each morning, and we're pretty busy the rest of the day."

"That's right," Nadia said. "I've only seen him a couple of times."

"Oh, okay," Jasmine said, her disappointment evident in her tone. "It's probably best anyway that I can't help out this week, since I'm already scheduled to work tomorrow and Saturday at the Sweet Stop." She shrugged. "But I'll see if I can adjust my hours for next week so that I work later in the day. Then I could volunteer with the camp...and maybe I'll see him at the ranch, too." Her switch from hopeless to hopeful in the span of two sentences reminded Maribeth of how she'd been at that age, seeing every glass as half-full.

Not anymore.

Maribeth felt certain she could keep Jasmine busy enough that she wouldn't have time to seek Ryan out, so she gave her a smile and said, "That sounds like a good idea. I'll put you down to help." She'd protect Jasmine from her infatuation. She had to. She couldn't bear to see her own history repeated with this sweet girl.

"Okay if I help again, too?" Nadia asked. "I really enjoy spending time with the kids and the Bible studies."

"Sure. We've got sixteen kids coming to the next camp, so I could use the extra help." Maribeth didn't mind the chance to spend more time with Nadia. Since she'd first moved to Claremont seven years ago, Maribeth had grown very close to the preacher's granddaughter. Brother Henry had been instrumental in bringing Maribeth back to God when she was certain He'd turned His back on her, and after she'd confided in the preacher about her mistakes, the kindhearted man had recommended that Maribeth work with the youth at the church and help them to stay away from the pitfalls she'd found herself in as a teen.

Maribeth had grown close to all of the kids, but Nadia and her friends, with their love of fashion and their love of God, held a special place in her heart. Often, the teen girls would visit Maribeth's store to shop, like Nadia and Jasmine were doing now, and they'd chat about God, life and boys. Not always in that order.

Today, though, Jasmine chose to skip talking about

boys in lieu of talking about men. One man in particular.

"It's just that he's so gorgeous. And he's here, in Claremont. Things like that don't happen every day. I mean, can you imagine dating someone like Ryan Brooks? Or, wow, marrying him? I mean, guys marry younger girls all the time, especially, you know, guys who are stars and everything. He's not a star like an actor, I don't guess, but you don't look like that and not be considered a star. And money. He's probably got more money than all of the star actors combined, don't you think? He is a Brooks, after all."

Maribeth cringed, remembering a time when she'd said something very similar and thought the whole world would be hers if she could date one particular man. But before she could spout some words of wisdom, Nadia beat her to the punch.

"Love isn't about money. It's about trust and faith, and about having your priorities right before anything else. You both need to love God, first and foremost." She gave Jasmine a silly smile. "And he's like, what, ten years older than you?"

Jasmine giggled. "Eleven. He's thirty, according to what it says under this photo. And it isn't like I've even talked to the guy, so I'm just saying that it'd be cool to marry him, not that I have any chance of it." Her smile crept into her cheeks and she lifted a blond brow. "But hey, if I did run into him, and if he happened to be smitten by me…"

Nadia playfully shoved her friend. "Come on. You've got to get to the Sweet Stop for work, and I've gotta go place another order for beads at Scraps and

Crafts." She nudged Jasmine, still grinning, toward the door. "I'll see you at the ranch tomorrow, Maribeth."

"And you might see Ryan there, too," Jasmine said.

Nadia shook her head and waved goodbye to Maribeth, and then the two girls headed out the door while Maribeth turned the volume up on the sound system piping out Christian music and allowed the lyrics to fill her head instead of the memory of the rich guy who dominated her past…and the reality of the one currently dominating her present.

Ryan shifted his hip in the passenger seat and prepared for more walking than he'd done in the past two weeks. Rehab was one thing; taking on the Claremont town square was something else entirely. But if he planned to get into full swing so he could get back to Chicago as soon as possible, he might as well get started.

Would a broken leg have kept his father away from the business this long? Probably not. Lawrence Brooks had only missed two days of work when Ryan and Dana's mother passed away. He hadn't even taken the time to mourn his wife; a broken leg and rehab certainly wouldn't have slowed the business magnate down. Then again, Ryan hadn't stopped running Brooks International. He'd held two conference calls today and seemingly kept to business as usual in spite of the distance.

Ryan grimaced. Why did he always compare himself to his father and find himself coming up short? Maybe because the media found the task so easy? They were quick to point out that the newest Brooks CEO merely followed his father's proven path for success. The statement that'd been penned by a reporter at the

Chicago Tribune had been picked up by practically every business magazine and summed up the public's interpretation:

"Though the company continues to hold its own, Ryan Brooks has brought nothing original to the stellar real estate empire founded by his father, the late Lawrence Brooks."

"Did you even hear what I said?" Dana asked, and Ryan realized he hadn't heard anything she'd said since they'd passed the tiny city-limit sign.

"Sorry, had my mind on something else," he said. "Repeat the question?"

She sighed. "It wasn't a question. I said that I can't believe we've never taken you to the square before." Dana pulled into a parking spot behind a row of brick buildings. Judging from the store names hand painted above each door, this was the back side of one section of the square. "But usually you come and go so quickly that we don't have time."

"Yeah, getting thrown from a horse extends a visit. Go figure." He wondered how big this town square was and how long it'd take them to deliver camp materials to Maribeth, his sister's purpose for the impromptu outing.

Dana laughed. "I do want longer visits from you, but I'll try to find another way to make that happen. And John warned you that Onyx might not be ready to ride." She grabbed her purse and the craft supplies from the backseat. "Then again, telling you that you can't do something is about the same as waving a red cape in front of a bull, isn't it? You've never been able to back down from a challenge."

"A challenge is merely another chance to prove

something that someone else thought impossible simply hadn't been done yet," he said.

Dana had her hand on the car handle but stopped her exit. "You sound just like him, you know."

Ryan didn't have to ask whom she referred to. He could almost hear their father's voice echoing each word as he'd spoken. "He gave us a lot of good advice."

"And before he died, he realized that his priorities were out of whack," she said. "I've told you before, he changed in those last days. I think if he could've talked to you one more time, he'd have probably pulled a one-eighty on a lot of that advice you're still following."

Ryan didn't want to hear about Lawrence Brooks's final days again when, according to Dana, he'd changed his mind about life, business and faith. Basically, he'd wished he'd done everything the opposite of the way he had. But Lawrence Brooks had single-handedly built a *Fortune* 500 company, and while Dana had stayed with their dad during his last days, Ryan had kept that company running. Still kept it running, in fact. So their father had done something right, and Ryan would keep that something going.

He opened his mouth to tell her that he suspected their father's change of heart had to do with the fact that he was heavily medicated at the time, but she shook her head.

"I know what you're going to say, and I don't want to hear it. One day you'll understand. But for now, forget I said anything." She climbed out of the car and hurried around to Ryan's side to help him exit, but he'd already opened the door, slowly maneuvered his straight leg out and then pushed his way up to the crutches.

"I've got it," he said, "but thanks."

Her mouth slid to the side, and she stepped a little closer, blue eyes that mirrored his own examining him as he balanced on the crutches. "I've missed you, Ryan. And there's so much more I want to show you, talk to you about, help you to see."

"We've got the whole afternoon. I promised not to work any more today, remember?" He knew she was ready to start preaching to him again, but he didn't want an intense conversation about life and faith. Not today. Maybe not ever.

Her eyes dimmed and her smile slipped a little. "Yeah, I remember."

Ryan knew she wanted him to stay here at least until his rehab ended in four weeks. But Lawrence Brooks wouldn't have stayed away from his business this long, and Ryan wouldn't, either. He wanted to make a name for himself the way his father had instead of piggy-backing on his father's success, and he couldn't make a name for himself staying in Claremont. "I want to make a difference," he said, more to himself than to Dana.

Her gasp should've warned him that the hug would follow. She wrapped both arms around him. "Oh, Ryan, that's what I've been praying for, and that's what Daddy figured out in the end. There's more to life than money and things. More to life than business."

She'd misunderstood, and Ryan had to set the record straight.

"No, Dana, I mean that I want to make a difference in business. Let *my* name be known. Achieve success for myself, instead of because I'm my father's son." He took a deep breath, let it out. "I should get back to Chicago. I can finish my rehab therapy there."

She released him from the hug and pressed a hand

to her forehead, spread her fingers and massaged her temples. Then she slid her hand to her throat and said, "Thanks to technology, anything you can do in Chicago can be done here. Didn't you say that today's board meeting ran even smoother with the teleconferencing system?"

"It did," he said, "but…"

An elderly gentleman stepped out of the rear entrance of a store labeled Tiny Tots Treasure Box carrying a bulging white trash bag. He nodded toward them as he dropped it into a nearby Dumpster and then grinned when he recognized Ryan's sister. "Dana! Good to see you. Are you coming to the toy store?"

She blinked a couple of times, dropped her hand from her throat and appeared to gain her composure before answering, "Not today, Mr. Feazell. But I'll visit you in a few weeks to get Abi's birthday present."

"You do that," he said. "And I'll help you pick out something nice." He then turned his attention to Ryan. "I heard you were in town again, Mr. Brooks. I met you at the wedding, of course, but you met a lot of folks that day. I've been praying for you while you recover. I reckon you know Dana put you on the prayer list at church. Looks like you're doing better," he said with another grin. "Prayers are working."

"I guess they are," Ryan said, and hoped this wouldn't start a religious discussion. Dana was already all geared up for preaching, but Ryan wasn't in the mood for a sermon.

Thankfully, the older man simply nodded his agreement and then returned to the marked door. "I'll see you at church Sunday, Dana," he said, and then to Ryan, "We'd love to see you there, too."

Ryan smiled but didn't commit to anything, then turned to his sister to see her smirking. "What?" he asked.

"Just thinking how cool it is to watch God work," she said.

"Aren't we supposed to be delivering some camp materials?" he asked.

She opened her mouth to say something but then snapped it shut, which told Ryan that he probably didn't want to hear whatever she'd been about to say. Then she turned, pointed toward the alley leading to the square and said, "Come on, I'll show you the way to Maribeth's store."

And just like that, his attention turned from their difference of opinion over their father's change of heart to the intriguing woman who'd been hovering in his thoughts for days—equally unsettling. Ryan couldn't put his finger on the reason Maribeth Walton had such an effect on him. Yes, she was beautiful, but he was often around beautiful women and had dated some of the most striking ladies in the world. Maybe her coolness toward him, her apparent apathy toward his status, piqued his interest.

But for whatever reason, Ryan had a serious attraction toward the woman they were going to meet, the kind of magnetism he'd only experienced once before, when Nannette securely captured his heart and then shattered it while the whole world read about the escapade in the tabloids.

Ryan refused to let that happen again. He'd maintain emotional distance when he and Dana saw Maribeth in a few minutes, and soon, he'd secure permanent distance between himself and the intriguing woman by going back to Chicago. Out of sight, out of mind, and all of that.

He needed to get back to his world, begin working on how to make his name stand out in the Brooks International empire and control the urge to lose his wits over another woman.

"Well, what do you think?" Dana asked when they exited the alley to find themselves in the midst of the box of buildings that comprised the Claremont town square.

Ryan scanned the unusual surroundings. "It's nice," he said. He had expected the square to take him back in time, but he hadn't anticipated how far, as though the entire town had been plucked from the 1950s and dropped in the middle of north Alabama. Very Mayberry.

A three-tiered fountain bordered by two mature oak trees centered the square, with children surrounding its edge tossing pennies into the sparkling water. Park benches dotted the grassy area around the fountain and held several elderly couples feeding squawking geese from bags of bread.

Elaborate eaves and fabric awnings decorated brick storefronts, and the majority of the shops had sidewalk displays to appeal to passing shoppers. There was a candy store, Mr. Feazell's toy store, a craft store, a barber shop complete with an old-fashioned striped pole, a five-and-dime, an art gallery, a bookstore, a sporting goods store and a shop titled Consigning Women. And *that* happened to be the place where his sister stopped, opened the door and waited for him to go inside.

This was where Maribeth worked?

A cool breeze met them upon entering, as did the

scent of apples and cinnamon, reminding Ryan of the woman who carried the same sweet scent.

Music filled the air. He didn't recognize the song, but the lyrics quickly told him it was a Christian tune. Then a clear soprano joined in from the back of the store as they made their way through the circular clothing displays.

Ryan took care not to knock anything down with his crutches while also studying the distinctive layout of the place. The clothes weren't merely hung on racks; they were arranged in ready-to-be-worn ensembles. Tops were paired with skirts and jewelry and shoes, everything a woman would need to match perfectly from head to toe.

While Dana paused to look at a red pantsuit, Ryan took a moment to examine the other original attributes of every outfit. Each one had a ribbon hanging nearby with an attached photo. Flipping over a photograph, Ryan saw a picture of Jennifer Aniston with a caption: "In February 2012, Jennifer Aniston chose a black-and-white chevron-print dress with leather accents for her movie's premiere. Paired with a black leather clutch, gold jewelry and black pointed-toe heels, her ensemble can be yours for $42.50."

"This is like Jennifer Aniston's outfit," he said to Dana.

His sister grinned. "And this one is like Kristen Stewart's. And that one is like Gwyneth Paltrow's." She pointed to a hot pink dress and strappy heels.

Ryan scanned the store and realized that there was only a small area noted as being for separates in the very back. All other space in the shop was filled with complete outfits. And beside the cash register, a huge wall collage featured countless photos of celebrities wearing clothes that were apparently available in this store.

"Maribeth has talent, doesn't she? To take an idea— for all women to be able to dress like celebrities— and then create a store to implement that idea?" Dana grinned at Ryan.

"She *owns* this place?" he asked, awestruck with the exceptional concept—a consignment store that recreated red-carpet looks.

Dana nodded as she moved to a bright yellow sundress and read the ribbon-embellished note. "Scarlett Johansson. I think I remember seeing her wear this." She scanned the pictures on the celebrity wall. "Yes, there she is. Do you think John would like this on me?" She checked the tag. "The size is right."

"Ingenious," Ryan said, marveling at the brilliant idea.

His sister held the dress against herself and viewed herself in a nearby elongated mirror. "I know. It's like having a personal stylist, but without the effort, or the price tag. Maribeth does all of the work, and it's a win-win. The folks bringing in items for consignment are happy because they sell more, and the ones buying the outfits are happy, too, because they can dress like the stars for a price that fits their budget. And her place is so popular that women drive all the way from Birmingham to get the look of a star for a price they can afford." She draped the yellow dress over her arm and grabbed the accompanying red jewelry. "Pretty incredible idea, don't you think?"

Ryan nodded and wondered if the woman realized the potential of her idea. She was sitting on a gold mine.

"We should probably go tell her we're here," Dana said, pointing toward Maribeth, who swayed as she held coral jewelry against a royal blue dress. She'd tacked a photo to the wall nearby and checked the dress against the picture, a photograph from the newest issue of *People* magazine that featured Pippa Middleton wearing a similar dress and jewels.

Maribeth wore a sleeveless black dress with a thin red belt and sky-high red heels. An assembly of gold bangles traveled up and down her delicate arms as she attached the necklace to the blue dress and then reached for the earrings. Her voice blended with the music, this song about blessings, and when Dana tapped her shoulder, she jumped, let out a high-pitched yelp and tossed one of the earrings in the air.

"Oh, my," she said, gasping. Red-tipped fingers fluttered beneath her slender throat. "I didn't hear you come in." She laughed, leaned down and scooped up the discarded earring, then seemed to notice Dana wasn't alone. "Oh, hello."

Ryan didn't miss the change in her tone, as though she weren't quite happy with his arrival in her store. Then again, this wasn't a store for guys. "Hello," Ryan said. He'd decided to maintain his distance from the woman, but her fascinating concept captivated him. He wanted to know more. "You put all of these outfits together, based on what celebrities wear?"

She'd seemed cool at first, but her face lit up with the question. "And based on what customers turn in for consignment, of course. Do you…" She paused. "Well, what do you think of the store?"

"It's brilliant," he said honestly. He saw Dana's broad grin from the corner of his eye, but he didn't care. It *was* brilliant, and the lady deserved to know. This was the type of thing that stood out—a great idea, innovative concept. *This* was the kind of thing that put your name on the books. "Have you thought about taking the idea bigger, beyond a single store? This is the only one so far, I take it?"

"Yes, it is," she said, the coolness returning to her tone, "and no, I *don't* want to go bigger." Then she dismissed the conversation with a pivot toward Dana. "That yellow dress will look gorgeous on you. Did you see the shoes that go with it? They're a size six. Isn't that your size?"

"It is," Dana said, "and I didn't see the shoes. I'll want them, too, I'm sure. But I don't know how much wear I'll get out of the dress." She placed a hand on her stomach. "Should be showing in the next month or so, I think."

Maribeth placed her hands together beneath her chin. "Well, you can wear it up until then, and it'll be perfect next summer after the baby's born."

Dana grinned. "I like the way you think. So, where are those shoes?"

"They're on top of the clothing rack," Maribeth said, stepping around Ryan to retrieve the red pumps and then showing them to Dana while still keeping her back to him. "What do you think?"

"I'll take them," Dana said. "But my main reason for coming to the store today wasn't to shop. I got those craft supplies for you from the church and thought I'd drop them off so you'd have them for tomorrow." She handed the plastic bag of supplies to Maribeth.

"You could've waited and given them to me in the morning." Maribeth continued to look directly at Dana as she spoke, as though Ryan wasn't even in the store. What was it about this woman and ignoring him?

Ryan continued to scan the store, the layout, the concept. *Brilliant,* his mind continued to whisper. His skin bristled with excitement, with the endless possibilities. This…was exactly what he needed.

Dana shrugged. "Ryan has only left the ranch to go to rehab, and I thought he'd like to see the square since he hasn't been here before." She shifted the dress to her other arm and ran her fingers across the fabric.

"Okay." Maribeth looked skeptical, and Ryan also thought Dana seemed to be stretching her reasoning to the limit. If he didn't know better, he'd say she brought him to this specific store to watch her friend give him the cold shoulder again. Or maybe because she'd detected the unwanted attraction that he felt toward Maribeth.

From the gleam in Dana's eyes, he'd hit the mark.

That attraction could get Ryan in trouble. The situation, the feeling he got when he was around her, the fact that she didn't seem to care whether he noticed her or not…were all so similar to the way his relationship had started with Nannette.

But Ryan was going to have to control the attraction this time, because he couldn't ignore a concept that might very well provide his means of putting his own stamp on Brooks International. A consignment store that specialized in making the less fortunate feel and look rich. This was the kind of thing that made a difference and exactly what Ryan had been looking for.

Maribeth and Dana chatted about the upcoming camp activities, and Ryan noticed the dark-haired beauty didn't even glance his way as she spoke.

"The kids are going to love this," she said, squaring her shoulders so that she clearly blocked Ryan from the conversation. He couldn't recall whether he'd ever been so thoroughly ignored.

Dana continued speaking, but lifted a brow and fought a grin. "I think so, too."

Ryan was used to people hanging on his every word, which was probably why her disregard hit him like a slap in the face. And made him even more determined. He'd had enough. One way or another, the lady was going to pay attention to him. He didn't pull off running an international business by not knowing how to get people to pay attention. He simply had to say something she couldn't ignore. Undoubtedly she didn't like the idea of growing her business, which baffled Ryan. Why wouldn't anyone want to take what they had and make it better? Bigger? More profitable? He'd find out, but first he had to get her to speak—period. And he'd already established her primary interest, so he capitalized on that knowledge.

"So, Maribeth, whose outfit are you wearing today?" he asked, causing the two women to stop talking and look his way.

Unable to ignore a question directed specifically to her, she turned, lifted an arched brow and asked, "Whose outfit?"

For a moment, he forgot his own question. When she looked at him directly, Ryan found himself lost in the appreciation of eyes that looked like melted chocolate, dark hair pulled up on the sides yet still reaching her waist and a mouth that made him wonder whether her lips were as soft as they appeared.

"Ryan?" Dana prompted.

Thankfully, his brain kicked back into play. "Which celebrity are you wearing today? That is what you do here, isn't it? Match the items you receive to celebrity ensembles?"

An enthusiasm claimed her exquisite face, the passion for her idea shining through as she answered, "Yes, it is." She smoothed a hand down the side of her dress. "This one is modeled after an outfit Reese Witherspoon wore on Letterman."

"I like it," Dana said.

So her wall of resistance cracked a little when he brought up her business. Good to know. And talking about business also kept his mind focused on his goal, instead of on the attraction that he'd have to control. "I like it, too," he added, and realized that she became even more appealing when her cheeks blushed bright pink.

Dana stared at the two of them with a triumphant smile, which only reinforced Ryan's stance to control this bizarre attraction. "I'll take the outfit," she finally said, and the two women moved to the cash register so Maribeth could ring up the sale.

Ryan took his time moving toward the checkout area. He wanted to see as many of the ensembles as possible along the way to verify that they were all as interesting and unique as the ones he'd already viewed. They were, and he also noticed that they weren't merely modeled after the younger starlets. Maribeth also had clothing designed to model Meryl Streep, Diane Keaton and Susan Sarandon. Her store had no age restriction. Ingenious.

Ryan got to the checkout area at the same time that Dana said, "I just wish Ryan would stay here until his rehab is complete. He told me a little while ago that he was thinking about leaving and finishing up his therapy in Chicago."

Maribeth's eyes lit up, and she turned her attention to Ryan as he took the last couple of steps to the counter. "Well, I'm sure you'd be more comfortable at your own place," she said, sliding the dress, shoes and jewelry into a garment bag.

If Ryan didn't know better, he'd say the woman was inwardly celebrating his departure. But what she didn't realize was that Ryan thought he'd found a way to make his mark on Brooks International, and it involved her unique idea. More than that, he knew that he couldn't convince her to partner with Brooks International from Chicago.

"I've changed my mind about heading back home. I'm going to stick around for a while and finish up my initial treatments in Claremont."

"Really?" Dana beamed. "Oh, Ryan, that makes me so happy!"

He grinned, finding it interesting that Maribeth's pretty mouth fell open into a silent "Oh" with his announcement. And if he'd looked back before exiting with Dana, he was sure he'd have seen an accompanying "No."

Good thing he liked a challenge.

Chapter Two

At just past 7:00 a.m., Maribeth turned onto the driveway beneath the wooden sign identifying the Cutter Fish Camp and Dude Ranch. In the spring, when Brother Henry announced the need for volunteers with the church camps held at the ranch over the summer, Maribeth had jumped at the chance to not only help Dana but also work with a group of kids in a Christian environment.

However, she hadn't counted on Ryan Brooks being part of the equation. And she still had three weeks to go in her commitment to volunteer the entire month of June. Based on what he'd said last night, he'd be here for all three of those weeks plus another one. Four more weeks of therapy, which meant four more weeks of Maribeth being around a guy who reminded her of her worst mistake.

God, are You trying to teach me some lesson here? Because I'm pretty sure I've already learned this one. Or are You giving me a temptation I'm supposed to overcome? Is that it? Because if it is, I want You to know that I'm not tempted to make the same mistake again. And it'd suit me just fine if You'd go ahead and give Ryan the desire to go home. He doesn't tempt me at all.

She rounded the last curve in the driveway and saw the non-temptation tossing slivers from a bale of hay over the fence toward the black stallion. His crutches were propped nearby, and he apparently had his weight settled on his good leg so he could fling the slices of hay farther. The action caused his biceps to flex against the sleeves of his navy T-shirt, and Maribeth was pretty sure she also noticed a couple of indentations in the front of that shirt where a six-pack, or maybe eight-pack, of abs were also in steady motion. His jeans were ripped along the outer seam to allow room for his cast, which only added to the entire rugged image.

So *this* was what she got for arriving earlier than usual. She'd hardly seen Ryan Brooks here since Monday, because typically he had gone to his therapy session by the time she arrived. But today she'd wanted extra time to get the additional materials ready for her two new campers. And because of her efficiency, she had no choice but to start her day interacting with America's most eligible bachelor billionaire.

Lovely.

He tossed the last shard of hay across the fence, then shook his head at Onyx, who was holding his nose in the air as if he didn't want the treat. "Your stubbornness is only making me more determined," Ryan said, then turned his back on the horse, which put him facing Maribeth.

She was still in the car but her window was down, so she couldn't ignore him when he asked, "You need help carrying anything?"

Great. He was injured and still attempting to feed a horse and assist Maribeth with her camp supplies. "No, I'm good," she said. She actually had quite a lot of supplies to carry into the barn, but having him help her tote them would only put him in closer proximity than he already was, and she didn't need or want to be any closer to the man. Really.

She scooped up the bag of materials Dana had brought her last night, as well as a container filled with trail mix she'd made this morning for the group. Then she looped her other arm through her purse and shifted to open the door, while the gorgeous rich boy leaned against the fence eyeing her slow progress.

The car door opened partially and then started back on her before she got all the way out, slamming her shin. "Ouch!"

He reached for his crutches.

"No, I've got it," she said through gritted teeth.

With a grunt, Ryan let go of the crutches, then leaned against the fence again. "Looks like Onyx isn't the only stubborn one around here," he said.

Maribeth wanted to reply with some snappy remark, but the sight of him caused all form of speech to lodge in her throat. His arms were crossed, drawing attention to those muscular biceps and a hard-plated chest. Add to that eyes that appeared even bluer in the morning sunlight and a smile that looked more genuine than confident, and—billionaire or not—he could be the poster guy for every woman's temptation.

And that included Maribeth.

Okay, God. So I was wrong. He's tempting. But I can handle it. I'm not going to fall for a guy like him

*again. But even so, if You don't mind, make it easier
on me and send him home.*

With all of her materials balanced in both arms, she
kicked the car door closed and started toward the barn
the same way she did every morning, except that there
was no way to get there without walking near the guy
leaning against the fence and grinning.

Did You have to make him so *good-looking, Lord?*

She took a deep breath, let it out and asked, "Something funny?" Then she silently reprimanded herself
for her snarky tone.

"Nooope," he drawled, and she suspected he was
trying hard to sound country. He pulled it off fairly
well, but she wouldn't tell him that. "I'm just enjoying
this amazing morning," he said. "Some sky, isn't it?"
He tilted his head toward the fields, and for the first
time today, Maribeth absorbed her surroundings beyond the appealing rich guy.

The green fields had a golden hue as the sun began
its ascent and bathed the grass in yellow light. White
Charolais cattle gathered in several groups on the
nearest hills like earthbound clouds; Fallon, Red and
the other docile horses huddled near the barn, apparently waiting for John to bring out a fresh round of
sweet feed. A rooster crowed in the distance, chickens
clucked, cows mooed and horses neighed, each sound
adding to the appeal of the scene, as did the combined
smells of hay, worn leather and sweet feed.

But Ryan's comment about the sky pulled her attention away from the normal sights, sounds and smells of
a morning on the farm to the reddish-orange hue claim-
ing dominion above the colors of the land. "Wow," she
whispered.

He nodded. "I've never seen a sky that red in Chicago, but that could be because the smog from the city covers it up. Either way, this one is pretty incredible."

She couldn't argue with the truth. "Yeah, it is."

"What's that saying?" he asked. "Something about red skies at morning?"

Still captivated by the scene, Maribeth quoted, "'Red skies at night, sailors delight; red skies at morning, sailors take warning.' It's actually taken from a verse in the Bible. I believe it's in Matthew."

"I wouldn't know about whether it's in the Bible," he said, "but I have heard the saying before."

His honesty about his lack of Bible knowledge took her by surprise. In this area of the country, "the buckle of the Bible Belt," as it was called, most everyone was at least familiar with what was or wasn't in the Good Book. And if you didn't know that much about it, you sure wouldn't readily admit it. But Ryan appeared nonchalant about his admission. As if it were no big deal.

Maribeth suddenly thought she knew why God put this man in her path. It wasn't to tempt her; it was because she was meant to help him. "We have a Bible study here every day of the camp. I'll probably use that verse in the one we have this afternoon. If the weather does get bad, we'll have the Bible study in the barn instead of on the trails, so you could come." A sense of rightness filled her with the invitation. He might have everything money could buy, but he apparently didn't have God in his life. And she knew what a difference He could make.

Ryan seemed to consider her words but then shook his head. "I don't think so. I've got several conference calls scheduled for this afternoon and reports to review."

Maribeth had no doubt the head of the company could adjust his schedule if he wanted, and clearly, Ryan didn't want to.

"So we're in for some bad weather?" he asked.

She decided it best not to push the Bible study request. If she was meant to get him thinking about God, she'd do it slowly and patiently. Maybe she could control the temptation of having Ryan Brooks around if she were focused on introducing him to the Lord. "I didn't watch the weather report," she admitted, "but if the saying holds true, then yeah, I guess we are. And I've never known the sky to be wrong about that. My daddy actually gauges his fishing trips in the Gulf around the sky more than the weather report."

"Your father goes deep-sea fishing?" he asked.

"It's a popular thing to do where we live—where they live, I mean," she corrected.

"Where's that?" he asked.

"In Destin, Florida, where I grew up. We ate a lot of fresh seafood that he caught on his weekend fishing trips. Daddy works for an office supply company during the week, but he lives for the weekends when he can go fishing. And whenever our friends and family came to town, they usually wanted to go fishing with Dad."

"My father and I talked about deep-sea fishing together sometime, but we never got around to it." He opened his mouth as if he were going to say more, but then stopped and took his attention back to that crimson sky. "So you grew up at the beach?"

"We didn't live on the beach, but we were very close, walking distance," she said.

"I've always heard people who grow up on a coast never leave. And your family is still there?" Those blue eyes returned their focus to Maribeth, and she felt oddly uncomfortable in the way he studied her, as though he were trying to put the pieces of her past into place.

She'd rather her past stay put where it was, but she wasn't going to ignore his question. "Yes, they're still in Destin."

"Are you close to your family?" he continued.

Maribeth glanced toward the log cabin and wished Dana would come on outside to get her out of this conversation. "Yes, I am," she said, and when he looked as though he doubted it, she added, "I love my parents and my two sisters very much, and I didn't leave Destin to get away from them, if that's what you're implying."

He lifted his palms. "Hey, I didn't mean to imply anything. I'm just making conversation." Then he smiled, and Maribeth tried to relax. He was making typical getting-to-know-you conversation, and she'd had these same questions asked several times when she first moved to Claremont. Yet somehow having Ryan Brooks ask them seemed too personal.

Be polite, she silently told herself. This was Dana's brother, after all, and he couldn't help it if *he* was so very similar to the actual reason she'd left Destin.

"What made you leave the beach for a town like Claremont? Since you own your store, I'm assuming you could've started it in Destin, or in any other town. I'd never even heard of Claremont until Dana met John Cutter. How did you find the place?"

She'd also been asked that question quite often when she first relocated to the tiny town, and even though she hadn't heard it in a while, she recited her trademark answer. "I wanted to experience life in a small town," she said, forcing a smile, "and I wanted to start a business on my own."

"Make a name for yourself?" he asked.

Actually, she'd been running away from the name she'd made for herself. Making a *new* name for herself would be more like it. "Something like that," she said. Thankfully, she saw Dana walking toward the barn with a travel mug in each hand.

"I know what that's like," he said, "wanting to make a name for yourself."

Maribeth started to ask him what he meant, but then Dana called out, "Hey, Maribeth, I didn't know you'd be here already. I got a cup of coffee for me and Ryan. Want me to get you one, too?"

"I had a cup before I left the store, but thanks," Maribeth answered.

"You've already been to work this morning?" Ryan asked.

"I live there. That was one of the things so appealing about the place on the square—each store has an apartment on the second floor." She hadn't planned on saying more than a couple of words to the guy as she made her way to the barn, but oddly enough, she was finding him easy to talk to.

"Pretty cool, huh?" Dana asked as she reached them. "That Maribeth can simply walk downstairs to be at work?"

"Yes," he said, "it is."

Maybe this was God's way of showing her that she didn't have to see guys like Ryan Brooks as completely off-limits. He didn't have to be a temptation that she couldn't withstand. Maybe they could be friends and she could even help him with his relationship with God somehow. Then she could go her merry way without any form of discomfort from being around someone who so blatantly reminded her of her past mistakes.

"Wow, did y'all notice that sky?" Dana asked, taking a sip of her coffee.

"We were just talking about that," Ryan said. "And about that old saying that red skies in the morning mean bad weather is coming."

"Oh, that's right." She held up the other mug. "Want your coffee now, or you want to wait until we're in the car?"

"I'll wait," he said.

Dana nodded, still taking in that sky, which seemed to have grown even redder in the time since Maribeth and Ryan had started talking. "I'd forgotten about that red-skies-at-morning thing," Dana said.

"Apparently it comes from the Bible," Ryan said, and then he laughed when Dana sputtered on her coffee. "I only know because she just told me." He tilted his head toward Maribeth.

"Well," Dana said, "you have my permission to share any Biblical knowledge you want with my brother. I've been trying to introduce him to Jesus for a couple of years now, but he hasn't been interested."

"I asked him to the camp's Bible study this afternoon," Maribeth said, "but he's busy."

"I have conference calls," he repeated, "and I wouldn't have a thing to contribute to a Bible study." When Dana started to speak, he shook his head. "Don't, sis. We've gone through this before. That's your life, not mine."

Maribeth suddenly felt sorry for her friend. And she also felt sorry for her own family, when they'd tried to bring Maribeth back to the straight and narrow road and she'd barreled on her own way. Later, she'd regretted that. And she wondered if Ryan Brooks would regret it later, too. "You should at least give the Bible study a try," she said.

He grabbed his crutches and put one beneath each arm. "Like I said, I wouldn't know anything about it, and I'm not going to attempt to participate in something I know nothing about. But I do know a thing or two about business, and I'd like to talk to you sometime about yours. Consigning Women, the business—the concept—has a lot of potential, and you've only scratched the surface. I could help you make that name for yourself."

And just like that, Maribeth saw through the nice-guy image to the real man beneath the friendly facade. He'd seen her business and wanted it for himself. Maybe not the whole thing, but he had hopes of using her idea for his own benefit. She could see it in his eyes: another rich boy used to getting any and everything he ever wanted. He was being nice because he wanted something.

"I don't think so," she said, and didn't hide the irritation in her tone. Then she turned away, told Dana to have a good day and headed into the barn.

Ryan's coffee sloshed in the travel mug when Dana stomped on the brakes before they reached the main road.

"Hey, easy there," he said, taking a sip to keep more from spilling over the top.

"I don't get it," she said, apparently forgetting that they were already running late to his rehab appointment. "Maribeth told you last night that she isn't interested in her business growing bigger, but you just won't let up, will you?" She placed her mug in the cup holder and put the car in Park, obviously not going anywhere until Ryan responded.

"Why wouldn't anyone want to go bigger?" he asked.

"Everyone isn't you, Ryan," she said, then visibly swallowed. "Everyone doesn't want to be Dad." When he didn't say anything, she continued, "That's it, isn't it? You think you've got to spend your life trying to make everything a little bit better, and a whole lot bigger, the same way he did. Well, I'll tell you something. That didn't make him happy, because things couldn't satisfy him. He realized that in the end."

Ryan had heard this speech way too many times in the two years since Lawrence Brooks had died, and he didn't want to hear it again, particularly since it wasn't true. "I'm not trying to be Dad. That's the whole point of me wanting to help grow Maribeth's business. She said she came here to make a name for herself, and I understand that, because that's what I want to do. I'm drowning in Dad's shadow. Everything I've done at that company has been done exactly—*exactly*—the way Dad did it. Nothing original. Nothing new. I've followed his strategies, utilized his resources and basically continued living in his world. My investments, each and every resort property, were the ones he already had in his sights when he died. Do you realize that the board hasn't approved anything that he hadn't already set into play?"

"Nothing you've recommended to the board has been approved?"

"That's just it. I haven't had a chance to recommend anything, because Dad had the next decade lined up."

"How?"

"Not exact properties and investments, but he set the plan in motion, the types of scenarios that were must-have purchases for the company, and that's what the board is looking for. They aren't interested in messing with a system that works."

"But that leaves you out of the equation," she said.

"The one time they've deviated from Dad's plan was when they approved the funding for new entrepreneurs, and that was due to you going to bat for John's dude ranch."

"But you want to make *your* mark in the company as well, and you saw Maribeth's idea as a way to make that happen," she said, realization dawning on her face.

"Pretty much. Maribeth's idea is ingenious. She's tapped into something original, inventive and clever, and I think—no, I know—that I can help her make it huge. I'd be investing in something that *I* found, something that *I* believe in. Something Brooks International has never done before."

"But it's Maribeth's concept," she said. "And she likes it the way it is—a small store in the Claremont town square. She doesn't want to make it bigger."

"She said she wanted to make a name for herself," Ryan repeated.

"And she has, here, in Claremont." Dana ran her hand through her hair then turned to face him. "Listen, I know you think convincing her to hand over Consigning Women so that you can turn it into some worldwide conglomeration is a good idea and that deep down, you actually believe you'd be helping her."

"I would be."

"Not if it isn't what she wants." She shook her head, then said, "I thought, or rather, I hoped that part of your decision to stick around for the remaining weeks of your therapy was because you had an interest in Maribeth. And I don't mean her business, but her, the person. In my opinion, she's exactly the type of person you need in your life. She's beautiful and smart, and she loves God. And she's feisty enough to handle you, which I can't say about most women." She opened her fingertips above the steering wheel and then curled them in to clasp it, but Ryan suspected she'd rather be pressing them against his throat. She'd never been good at hiding irritation. "I thought you were acting interested in her, but I should have known you were only interested in her idea and what you could do with it."

Ryan didn't know what to say. He couldn't deny that he was physically attracted to Maribeth, but he also didn't plan on acting on that attraction. Dana was right; the lady was beautiful, smart and feisty. And she seemed like the real deal when it came to her love of God, which was something Dana wanted in Ryan's life, even if it wasn't something he was looking for. Truthfully, he didn't know enough about God to know whether he wanted Him in his life or not. But the main reason he couldn't have any type of relationship with the woman was because that strong, bizarre attraction he felt every time she was around seemed way too similar to the fascination he'd had toward Nannette. It felt real. And his past experience told him that if it seemed that real that quick…it wasn't.

He wouldn't get his heart broken again.

"Wait a minute," Dana said, studying him as though she knew his very thoughts. And, based on past experience, he suspected she did. All of those years with the two of them depending on each other as best friends when their father left them to one nanny or another had them so tuned in to each other's feelings that Dana didn't miss where his mind had headed now.

"You *are* feeling something toward Maribeth, aren't you?" she questioned. "But you're still suffering from shell shock after what happened with Nannette." She nodded once, as though she didn't need affirmation from Ryan to know she'd hit the mark. Then she picked up her coffee mug, took a sip and then put the car in drive. "I've changed my mind," she said, pulling out onto the road.

Ryan drank his coffee, which had turned cold and bitter, and debated whether to ask, but curiosity got the best of him. "Okay, I'll bite. Changed your mind about what?"

"About you talking to Maribeth about her business. I think you should try to convince her to let you help her out, make her business bigger and all of that." Her smile looked way too smug. "Yeah, I think that's a great idea, in fact."

He could figure out nearly every board member's wishes by studying their faces at the table, but he had no idea what was going on in Dana's mind right now. "You think it's a great idea?"

"Yes. Because I know Maribeth, and she isn't going to do anything she doesn't want to do. If she has her mind made up, there isn't a thing you can do to change that." Still grinning, she accelerated and added, "But I also know that she could make a difference in your life. Because she's exactly what you need, whether you realize it or not, and I'm not talking about her business."

"It's her business I'm interested in," he said. "That's it." But even as he said the words, he, like Dana, debated whether they were true.

Chapter Three

Ryan was more sore than usual after this morning's rehab, but based on what Dr. Aldredge had said, that was a good thing. And the doctor had finally unlocked the cast, so he could get around better and start wearing normal clothes. Though this apparel could hardly be considered normal for Ryan. Dana had bought him a few Western shirts during their trip to the square and insisted that he wear them to "blend" on the farm during his stay. She'd been so excited about buying them that Ryan didn't argue, but it still took him by surprise when he looked in the mirror and saw something like a "real" cowboy staring back at him.

The shirt was red-and-brown plaid. Plaid. Ryan had never worn anything plaid in his life, but Dana had liked it and said it was a "must-have," so he'd conceded. He couldn't recall owning a shirt that snapped instead of buttoned, either, but this one did. The saleslady at the Country Outfitter store had first wanted to take his picture so she could prove Ryan Brooks actually shopped there, and then she'd wanted another of him wearing some of the clothes. Ryan had obliged. He was used to people taking his picture, after all, even if it hadn't happened since he'd arrived in Claremont. But he also had to admit that it was nice not having a big lens pointed at him every time he went out.

However, the woman's exclamation that he should keep wearing the clothes because they made him "look just like Blake Shelton" got a laugh out of Ryan. He didn't have the foggiest idea who Blake Shelton was, though Dana quickly clued him in about the famous country singer. The thing was, Ryan had never bought—and would never buy—something to try to look like someone else. He was his own person. Or at least that's what he wanted to be, even if he often found himself lost in the memory of Lawrence Brooks. Like today, when the head of acquisitions for Brooks International questioned whether Ryan thought his father would have selected the resort Ryan had purchased last year in Miami. No, the return on investment wasn't where it needed to be yet, but that had more to do with the economy than the possibility that the purchase was a poor decision on Ryan's part.

He was proud of everything his father had accomplished, but tired of having every decision compared to the master. If he had a way to make his name known, put his personal stamp on the Brooks empire, then maybe his board would stop questioning his every move.

A crack of lightning brought his attention to the storm brewing outside. He'd spent the afternoon responding to corporate memos and evaluating the weekly reports, and he'd planned to get outside for a breath of fresh air when he finished. But the bad weather they'd anticipated had arrived, and from the look of things, it'd hit the campers on their way back. The line of horses moved slowly through the drizzle toward the barn, and even in the gray haze, he could see Maribeth's smile.

There was something so compelling about the woman, not merely because of her beauty but also due to her determination. She'd left her home and her family behind to pursue her dream in a brand-new town, and her store seemed to be doing as well as it could in the tiny place. More than that, she seemed satisfied with the slight measure of success. But Ryan had no doubt she could do much better, make a real name for herself, if she'd only let him help.

Why was she being so stubborn?

And something told him that it wasn't merely obstinacy holding the woman back. She'd left a decent-size town on the beach, which would have a surplus of tourists and therefore much more exposure for her store, to start her business in a town that didn't even warrant a spot on most maps. And she'd left her family behind, when they could potentially have helped her with her start-up.

Maybe her family had been too controlling, and Maribeth hadn't wanted to start Consigning Women in a location where they would have the ability to take over. And maybe she thought that Ryan would also take her control away if she allowed Brooks International to help her expand.

The group disappeared into the barn, and he wondered how long they'd be inside. Every day they had returned from the trails with just enough time for the kids to be picked up, and then Maribeth and her volunteers would leave. But today they'd come back earlier due to the rain. And the fact that they were basically trapped in the barn for the time being would give Ryan the opportunity to make his way out there and talk to Maribeth before she had a chance to climb in her car and drive away.

He wanted to tell her he could help her grow her business without taking away her control. She could make all decisions regarding how each entity should run, but Ryan would oversee the company's direction. And he'd show his board that he could do something his father would never have dreamed of—bolstering a unique consignment-store concept, of all things—and be equally successful in the endeavor. A win-win. Maribeth would make a name for herself, and so would Ryan.

But first he had to get her to agree.

He grabbed his crutches and started toward the door in spite of the rain picking up speed. He wasn't about to let a little rain—or a headstrong woman—keep him from his goal.

Maribeth had never known a red sky to be wrong, and the one Ryan had pointed out this morning proved to be no exception. As the vivid hue had foretold, clouds overtook the afternoon, and rain burst free before the campers made it to the barn. The kids were great, though, laughing and enjoying the break from the summer heat, even if they were drenched. Since this week's group came from the Claremont Community Church, which Maribeth attended, she'd known all of the kids before the camp started. But being with them this week, particularly when they discussed the Bible, had endeared them even more to Maribeth.

Maribeth gathered them in the barn for their end-of-day Bible study and varied her intended devotion to incorporate the weather. Sitting on a bale of hay with the kids surrounding her on saddle blankets, she read from Matthew, chapter seven. "'Therefore everyone who hears these words of mine and puts them into practice is like a wise man who built his house on the rock. The rain came down, the streams rose, and the winds blew and beat against that house; yet it did not fall, because it had its foundation on the rock. But everyone who hears these words of mine and does not put them into practice is like a foolish man who built his house on sand. The rain came down, the streams rose, and the winds blew and beat against that house, and it fell with a great crash.'" She looked around at the children's faces and was thankful that they seemed to be paying more attention to her than to the rain beating against the tin barn or the horses in stalls lining one side. "So, what was different about the wise man and the foolish man?" she asked.

Kaden Brantley, an adorable seven-year-old with blond hair and bright blue eyes, stuck his hand in the air and answered, "One was smart, and one wasn't?"

Nadia, standing behind the group, put a hand to her mouth to keep from laughing out loud, and Maribeth also refrained from laughing, because Kaden was completely serious.

"Yes, that's true," Maribeth said. "And what else was different, about where they chose to build their houses?"

Nathan Martin, an energetic nine-year-old with a contagious smile, answered, "The wise man built his on the rock so it would hold up in the rain, but the foolish guy didn't think about the rain, I guess, and so his fell."

"Good answer, Nathan," Maribeth said. "And here's the part people sometimes don't think about. While the wise man and the foolish man had differences in where they chose to build their houses, there was something about the two of them that was the same. And I think that's a big part of why Jesus told this particular story." A few of the kids frowned or slid their mouths to the side as they apparently tried to figure out the answer. "Can any of y'all tell me how they were the same?"

Autumn Graham, a beautiful nine-year-old with auburn hair and dark brown eyes, timidly raised her hand. "I think I know."

Maribeth smiled at the sweet girl. She hadn't spoken a lot during the week, but when she did contribute to the conversation, her answers were well thought out and intelligent, way beyond her age. "Okay, Autumn. What would you say was the same about the two men?"

She leaned forward and asked, "Is it that both of their houses were in the storm?"

Nadia smiled from behind the group, and Maribeth nodded. "Yes, Autumn, they *both* were in the storm. And what Jesus is showing us with the story is that if we have Him in our life then we're building our house on the rock, and when a storm comes, we'll be okay. If we don't have Him, then our house is on the sand, like that foolish man's, and when the storms come, it will fall. But He isn't talking about houses and rainstorms, like the one we have today."

Nathan's hand darted into the air again, but he didn't wait for Maribeth to call on him before he answered.

"He's talking about when we have a hard time, like if kids are being mean to us, or things like that, right?"

"Exactly," Maribeth answered, enjoying this precious group of children. They'd been so involved in the trail rides and adventure hikes, but they were equally involved with the Bible lesson that accompanied each day. "Jesus is letting us know that everyone will have storms in their life, or hard times, but if we have our faith in Him, then we can make it through the storms, like the man who built his house on the rock." She glanced around at the kids and was thrilled to see they were all still listening, which was good; their parents weren't due to pick them up for another ten minutes, and she wasn't sure how long their attention spans would hold out. So she decided to ask another question to spark interaction. "I know I've had storms in life—" she thought of one in particular "—that Jesus helped me get through. Can any of y'all think of storms that you have had in your life?"

For a moment, they were silent, and she thought she might have ventured too far in the kids-willing-to-share department, but then Matthew Hayes, a ten-year-old with an abundance of personality, shot his hand in the air and said, "I think I have a big storm every time I have to take a math test in school."

His twin, Daniel, nodded. "Yep, math is our storm. We're horrible at it."

"Math is a storm for me, too," Nadia said from the back. "Or rather, calculus. I've always liked English and science better."

"We don't like English, either," Matthew said.

Daniel laughed. "Definitely not English. Our favorite subject is PE."

"Well," Maribeth said, attempting to gather their attention again, since all of the kids were now discussing their least favorite school subjects, "now you can remember that when you face the storms, like math or English, you can ask Jesus to help you get through it." She glanced up when she heard a car outside, and that's when she realized Nadia wasn't the only one in the back of the group.

At some point, Ryan had entered the barn. He leaned against the wall, near the entrance, and he looked like something straight out of a movie…with a drop-dead-gorgeous cowboy playing the lead. In all of the photos she'd seen of him in magazines or online, he'd worn an expensive suit or tuxedo. Typically, the tabloids snagged pictures at red carpet premieres and elaborate corporate functions, and he had been dressed accordingly. But ever since he'd arrived in Claremont, he'd altered that look completely with basic T-shirts and jeans ripped to accommodate his cast, which wasn't a bad look, either. But this…the Western plaid shirt complete with snaps and a vintage-style yoke dampened from the rain, coupled with dark jeans and—catch her breath—boots…*this* took the already off-the-charts good looks that he was known for to something, well, *completely* off the charts.

Nadia drew Maribeth's attention away from the handsome rich-boy-turned-cowboy with an overly loud cough and, judging by the teen's smile, caught Maribeth's dropped-jaw expression. Maribeth's cheeks flamed, and she prayed Ryan didn't notice, but she couldn't make herself look his way again to verify. Instead, she focused on the kids, who were still chatting about their least favorite school subjects. Maribeth had a couple of minutes left before the camp day ended, so she attempted one last question. "Okay, I agree about those subjects being tough. Do y'all know other kinds of storms you or other kids your age have to face?"

When most of the kids shook their heads, Autumn lifted her hand again.

"Okay, Autumn. Go ahead," Maribeth encouraged.

Autumn timidly glanced around at the other campers, swallowed and then said softly, "I think when your mom dies, like mine did, then that's like a storm in your life. Even though I was only four and it's been five years since she went to heaven, I still remember her. My dad, grandmother and I were all sad—" she glanced at the hay-covered floor and then whispered "—for a long time."

Maribeth blinked and her throat tightened, overcome with emotion. "That was a storm," she said.

Autumn nodded, and then one corner of her mouth lifted in a half smile. "But then my dad met Hannah, my mom now, and we started going to church again and praying—" the other corner of her mouth joined the first "—and then there wasn't a storm anymore. I think some storms are like that. And I know Jesus helped us."

Maribeth's heart clenched in her chest. She had heard about Autumn's biological mother losing her life to breast cancer, and she also now remembered that the little girl had gone two years without speaking after her mother died. But to see Autumn now, with her tender smile and sweet spirit, doing so well, Maribeth had to agree. "I do think that was a storm in your life, and I am so glad that the storm has passed."

"Me, too," Autumn said, as a few parents, all running under umbrellas, darted into the barn to pick up their kids.

Nadia took over getting the children to their respective parents while Maribeth chanced a look at the guy still standing patiently near the entrance. And her heart clenched once again. Because Ryan was no longer looking at Maribeth. His full attention was on little Autumn, and his clenched jaw and compassionate eyes showed her that the little girl's story of her past storm had touched him the same way it'd touched Maribeth.

Which wasn't good. It was bad enough that Ryan Brooks looked the way he did and had such an effect on her senses merely from standing nearby wearing cowboy gear. Realizing that he also had a sensitive heart wasn't doing anything for Maribeth's already shaky willpower. And when his eyes met hers and she saw that they glistened with barely contained tears, she knew for certain.

Ryan Brooks was exactly…what she didn't need.

Chapter Four

Ryan had been introduced briefly to the majority of the parents who came to the barn to pick up their kids, either at John and Dana's wedding or at the town square. Many of them were now friends of his sister and all of them went to the church Dana and John attended. Maybe that was why they spoke to him as though they knew him personally.

The odd feeling he experienced around them reminded him that there weren't a lot of people in Ryan's world who actually knew him. Occasionally someone in the media would attempt to speak to him in a friendly manner, as though they were close, but Ryan knew better. They simply wanted the inside scoop on his company's investments.

Ryan wasn't used to someone being nice without having an ulterior motive. But all indications told him that was status quo for this tiny town, especially in the manner that they seemed so comfortable around the CEO of Brooks International.

"Good to see you again," a young woman said. She had shoulder-length brown hair and appeared a few years younger than Ryan, maybe twenty-seven. "Jessica Martin," she said, when she realized Ryan didn't recognize her. "I've met you a couple of times, but I'm sure it's difficult to remember everyone here when the majority of your time is spent in Chicago. I know Dana's happy you're in Claremont, though, even if it is only temporary. And I'm glad you seem to be doing better." She waved at another woman entering the barn. The lady waved back, said hello to the two of them and then continued toward her child. "We've had you on the prayer list at church ever since your accident," Jessica said.

"I appreciate that," he said.

"Hey, you can never get too many prayers, right?" she asked with another grin.

Ryan wasn't sure how to answer that question, but thankfully, she forged ahead and he didn't have to.

"It's great that you're getting out more. I saw y'all on the other side of the square last night. My husband and I had the kids at the Sweet Stop—the candy and ice cream shop—and I saw you and Dana coming out of the consignment store. Pretty neat place Maribeth has, wouldn't you say?"

"Yes, I would," he said. In fact, the potential for her store was the reason he was still in Claremont, but he wouldn't discuss that with this lady. He would, however, talk to Maribeth about it, after all of the kids were picked up.

"Walking around at the square was probably easier than getting around the farm, I suppose. Sidewalks aren't as difficult to navigate as the ground around here." She ran her shoe across a clump of hay to prove her point. "Especially today, with the rain and all."

"It is a challenge," he said. In fact, Ryan's crutches

had slipped twice on the damp earth during his journey to the barn, but now that he was here and getting a chance to talk to Maribeth, he considered the risk well worth it. The parents were steadily picking up the kids, and eventually, there wouldn't be anyone left but Ryan. No way for her to ignore him today.

The little blond boy Ryan recalled as Nathan rushed toward them. "Hey, can I try out the crutches? You know, practice with them, just in case I ever break a leg or something?" He looked from Ryan to Jessica. "Is that okay with you, Mom? If he says yes?"

She did one of those mini shakes of the head, as though his odd request wasn't anything unusual for her son. "Nathan, Mr. Brooks needs his crutches, and unless you're planning to break a leg anytime soon—and I sure hope you aren't—you don't need to practice." She laughed at the boy's exaggerated frown, then said, "Ryan, in case you haven't already met, this is my son, Nathan."

"Hey," Nathan said, his voice not nearly as chipper now that he'd lost hope of practicing with Ryan's crutches.

"Nice to meet you, Nathan," Ryan said.

"Nice to meet you," he answered, still glumly.

"Nathan, Lainey is waiting on us in the car, so we need to go anyway," Jessica said, then explained to Ryan, "Nathan's little sister was too young for the camp this year." Then she looked back to Nathan. "And she's been waiting all day to see you."

"O-kay," Nathan said. He reminded Ryan of himself at that age, on the days he'd wanted to do something fun and his father had been too busy working to incorporate the activity into his schedule. And that included during vacations.

Ryan smiled at the kid. "You're coming back here tomorrow for the last day of camp, right?"

"Yes, sir."

"So tomorrow, when you're done, find me. If it isn't raining, I'll let you have a go at the crutches. The rain makes it tough, even for me. But I'm not sure how much practice you'll be able to do. These are much bigger than any crutches you would have."

"And we're hoping you never need any," his mother interjected.

"Right," Nathan said, smiling again. "But it'll be fun trying."

Ryan laughed. The boy did remind him of himself. "Okay then, tomorrow you can practice."

"Yes!" Nathan fist-pumped air.

"I didn't hear a thank-you there," his mom said.

"Oh, right," he said. "Thanks!" Then he darted into the rain toward one of the parked cars.

"You never know what a nine-year-old boy is going to want to try," Jessica said, then added, "I appreciate you letting him. I know it doesn't seem like a big deal, but trust me, that'll be all he thinks about until tomorrow. Oh, and praying that the rain stops by then."

"I'm glad to do it," Ryan said, meaning every word. Then he noticed Maribeth watching the interaction. He looked toward her, and she quickly turned to say something to her teenage helper.

After saying goodbye to Jessica Martin, he waited as more parents arrived and retrieved their kids. Most of them said hello, and Ryan returned the greeting. He wasn't used to feeling a need to speak simply because you encountered someone on the street, but he'd noticed last night that you didn't meet someone in Claremont, even in passing, without acknowledging the interaction with some sort of salutation.

After ten minutes passed and almost all of the kids had been picked up, the teen who'd been helping Maribeth all week said her goodbyes. On her way out, she stopped near Ryan.

"I'm Nadia Berry," she said. "I've seen you, but we haven't actually met."

"Ryan Brooks," he said, and then added, "but I'm guessing you knew that already."

She smiled. "Everybody knows that, whether they're from Claremont or not. But I try to think of you as just Miss Dana's brother."

He laughed. "Thanks."

"I'm glad you came to the Bible study," she said.

"It was good." Ryan had never been to one before, so he didn't have anything to compare it to, but he'd been impressed at how much the kids had participated, especially the little girl who spoke at the end. And he decided not to tell Nadia that he hadn't come to the barn for the Bible lesson, that he'd come to force Maribeth to talk to him, which essentially forced him to attend the Bible study.

"If you liked the Bible study, you'd probably like visiting church, too. Maybe you could come sometime. My granddaddy is Brother Henry, the preacher," she said.

He wouldn't make any promises he didn't plan to keep. "Maybe."

"Well, have a blessed day. Looks like I'm about to

get wet!" She took a deep breath and then ran toward her car, squealing and laughing.

In the time the two of them chatted, all of the remaining kids had been picked up, except for the little girl who had touched Ryan's heart. Autumn stood near Fallon's stall, and he watched Maribeth give her a green apple to feed the palomino. Autumn's face lit up when the horse happily chomped the treat, but that was nothing compared to the way it brightened when the last parent ran, dripping wet and panting, into the barn.

"I'm sorry I'm late," she said breathlessly, pushing wet hair from her forehead as she quickly moved toward Autumn. "I stopped by your dad's office to visit and wasn't thinking about the drive taking a little longer in the rain."

"I enjoyed her staying," Maribeth said.

Ryan suspected that was partially because she didn't want the last child to leave...which would give her no choice but to talk to him.

"And Fallon really likes her," Maribeth added.

"She likes me because I'm giving her apples." Autumn ran her hand down the mare's nose.

"Yeah," Maribeth said, "that's true, too."

The lady smiled. "So, I take it camp went good today, even with the rain?"

"It was great," Autumn said. She turned away from the horse to face her mom. "And the Bible study was good, too. We talked about storms, and I talked about my first mom—" she looked at Maribeth, then her mom, and smiled "—and then about you."

The lady blinked and ran a hand along Autumn's cheek. "I can't wait for you to tell me all about it on the way home." She glanced toward Maribeth. "Sounds like a good Bible study."

Maribeth nodded. "It was."

Feeling as though he were invading the private conversation, Ryan shifted on his crutches, and the lady jumped a little, apparently just noticing that she, Maribeth and Autumn weren't the only ones in the barn.

"Oh, I don't know how I didn't see you there, Mr. Brooks."

"Please, call me Ryan."

She smiled. "Okay. I'm Hannah. Hannah Graham. My husband is Matt Graham. And I guess you've already met Autumn."

"We haven't actually met, but I was here when she talked about her personal storm during the Bible study, and I thought it was incredible that a girl so young could be so wise."

Maribeth nodded her agreement, and Autumn shrugged timidly, but smiled.

Hannah put her arm around her daughter and gently squeezed. "Yes, she is."

Ryan started to say more about his own storms in life and how he'd also lost his mother when he was young, but he didn't feel right sharing something so personal with people he'd just met, so he paused and said to Autumn, "I'm glad everything worked out so well for you."

She leaned into Hannah and whispered, "Thanks."

Then Hannah again thanked Maribeth for taking care of Autumn until she arrived, said goodbye to Ryan, and the two of them jogged through the downpour toward their car. Leaving Ryan alone with Maribeth.

Finally.

He waited for Hannah's car to leave, but unfortunately, the minute it did, the rain came down harder than before, and he wondered whether Maribeth would be able to hear him over the water beating against the tin roof and the horses fidgeting in their stalls.

He'd wanted to convince her to let him grow her business, and he'd been eager for this opportunity. But now, with the rain echoing through the barn, and the woman he hadn't stopped thinking about all week standing in front of him, Ryan's throat closed in, the way it did when he was a freshman struggling through his first speech class.

He swallowed. He'd been the keynote speaker for at least a half dozen events in the past year, many of which had had nearly a thousand attendees, and without breaking stride had taken over command of a *Fortune* 500 company's board table when his father died. He'd never felt anything but excitement about each opportunity.

So why was he sweating now?

He shook off the ridiculous nerves, moved closer to her and said, "I've been wanting to talk to you."

Maribeth didn't know whether Ryan stepped closer because of the loudness of the rain or because he wanted to intimidate her a little, but in either case, she wouldn't let him think that he made her nervous. Even if he did. She took a small step toward him and said, "What a coincidence. I want to talk to you, too."

That strong jaw flexed, his brows raised a fraction and his beautiful mouth lifted on one side. And Maribeth didn't like the fact that she thought of his mouth as beautiful.

"Okay then," he said, his voice as deep and strong as she remembered, and sending a little tremor down her spine, "Ladies first."

She refused to be intimidated. She'd seen his high-and-mighty wall slip a little, and she wanted to know what had touched him earlier. "Why did you react that way to Autumn's story?"

The hint of a smile he'd had a moment ago flattened, and his jaw tensed again. "React?" he asked.

She knew she was onto something, and she wasn't going to stop until she found out what it was. "Don't try to act like I'm making this up. I saw you. You were touched by what she had to say."

"And you were, too, and Nadia, and probably several of the kids. She had a moving story." He shrugged. "She's a little girl who has been through a tough situation. Anyone would react to it."

Maribeth shook her head. "There was more to it than that."

He didn't answer, and his eyes moved to the stalls, where the horses were antsy about the storm.

Maribeth nodded once. "Okay then. That's fine. But you should know, I'm not interested in talking about whatever you want to talk about if you aren't willing to talk to me." She checked her jeans pocket for her car keys, felt them inside and then stepped around him. "Have a good day, Mr. Brooks." She wasted no time getting out of the barn.

The rain was much colder than it'd been earlier and slapped her face as she made her way to her car without looking back. But that didn't keep her from hearing him yell.

"Wait!"

Maribeth opened the car door and hurried inside, then slammed it to keep out any sounds in case he tried to stop her again. She'd pretend she didn't hear him and leave.

But a movement near the barn caught her eye, and she looked back to see Ryan on his crutches in the downpour moving directly toward her car.

"What are you doing? Are you craz—" She halted the words she knew he couldn't hear when she saw him hit a muddy patch of earth, his crutches sliding out from under him, and Ryan Brooks, the guy frequently hailed in the media as "larger than life and unstoppable," came crashing to the ground.

Maribeth jumped out of her car. She'd watched her steps as she'd left the barn to keep clear of the massive puddles forming around the barn entrance, but this time she didn't look down, her feet and ankles sinking into water as she made her way to the guy now lifting his head and squinting at her through the rain.

She knelt next to him and surveyed the damage. "Are you okay? What's hurt?" she asked, ignoring the water pouring around them.

Somehow his eyes looked even bluer as he peered up at her and grinned. "My pride?"

Relief flooded her like the water drenching them now. "Well, that's good, I guess," she said. "Here, let me help you up."

He pushed against the ground while Maribeth slid her arm around him to help him sit up. His shirt was soaked, and because of that, she easily felt the firm muscles of his back pressing against her arm. She swallowed past the sensation, waited until she was certain he had his balance and then pulled her arm away.

She'd almost forgotten about his broken leg, and she glanced at it now but couldn't tell if anything was wrong because of the jeans over his cast. "Your leg. Is it okay?"

"Hurts like—" He visibly swallowed and then that corner of his mouth lifted again and he answered. "Like, a lot," he said. "But I don't think I did any additional damage, at least not to the leg. I'm pretty sure that's no longer usable, though." He nodded toward one of his crutches, which Maribeth now saw had broken during his fall.

"Oh, my," she said, as a crack of thunder caused her to flinch. She reached for the other crutch, also lying a distance from its owner, and said, "I'll help you to the house. Can you make it with one crutch, if I help?"

He looked doubtful.

"I'm stronger than I look," she said, again putting her arm around him to help him stand and willing herself to stop enjoying the proximity. "Come on. We can do this."

He took the good crutch and used it and Maribeth as leverage to stand. The rain refused to cooperate and actually seemed to come at them head-on as they started toward the cabin.

Ryan's height caused him to lean awkwardly against her, and their progress was slow, which only increased the intensity of having him so near. Added to the sporadic cracks of thunder that caused her to reflexively hang on to him tighter, Maribeth started to wonder whether she should've left Ryan in the mud and called someone else to help. Normally, Dana and John or Georgiana and Landon would be here, but they'd all taken Abi to a horse show in Atlanta this morning.

So Maribeth was on her own. And it wouldn't have been right to leave him there, no matter how difficult this journey to the cabin was on her senses.

Help me, Lord. I know You're in control of this, and for some reason, You've got me in this difficult situation. Help me be strong and keep those old feelings at bay. I don't need a guy like him. I don't need a repeat of the past.

By the time they reached the ramp, Maribeth felt soaked to the bone. Her body shivered, and although Ryan undoubtedly tried to keep the majority of his weight on the other crutch, her shoulder ached from helping him balance. Thankfully, the ramp had a rough-textured surface, and Ryan's crutch didn't slip at all as they made their way to the shelter of the porch.

"I'll be fine there, for now," he said, pointing to the nearest rocker.

"Don't you want to go inside and get dry?"

"I will, in a minute. First I want—I need—to talk to you." He urged her toward the rocker, and with Maribeth moving out of the way, he sat down.

Her tremble was instantaneous, a frisson that might have been caused by the cold rain or by the removal of Ryan's warmth against her side.

"Here," he said, reaching toward a cedar chest not far from his chair and opening it to withdraw a blanket. "Use this to warm you up."

"I really should go, and you need to get inside and change into dry clothes."

"I'm all right," he said, "but if you want some dry

clothes, you could borrow some of Dana's. I'm sure she wouldn't mind." He took a deep breath. "And I don't want you to go," he said softly. "Not yet. Like I said, I've been wanting to talk to you."

"I don't need to borrow any clothes. The blanket is fine." She wrapped it around herself and sat in the next rocker. "But I did mean what I said about talking to you. You have to answer me before I'm going to feel any kind of obligation to answer you."

He nodded as if he'd expected her stance. "Okay."

She'd started rocking, but she stopped. "Okay?"

"I want you to hear me out, and if I have to talk first, then I'm ready. What was it you wanted to know?"

His tone said he hoped she'd forgotten, and he wasn't going to boost her memory. But she hadn't.

"Why did you react so strongly to Autumn's story, when she talked about her storm?" As if reinforcing the question, an earsplitting crack echoed through the woods—lightning striking nearby. She wrapped the blanket around herself tighter.

"I reacted so strongly," he said, his words measured and gauged as though controlling the emotion behind them, "because her story, her storm, so closely resembled mine."

Maribeth wouldn't have thought he had anything in common with the little girl, but then she thought about Autumn's story and recalled Dana mentioning her mother, and that she'd died giving birth to Dana. "She lost her mother when she was young, and you did, too," she said.

"She said she was four. I was three." He didn't look at Maribeth as he spoke but stared toward the fields instead. Maribeth followed his line of sight to see the black stallion in the distance, the only animal that hadn't attempted to get out of the storm. And she thought of Autumn in her storm, and Ryan in his. "That was tough on you, wasn't it? Losing your mom so young?"

He continued focusing on the stallion, but Maribeth noticed his hands gripping the wooden armrests on the rocker and his throat pulsing thickly as he swallowed. Then he said, "I think because I was so young, losing her wasn't the toughest part." He turned toward Maribeth and she saw the depth of suffering, of loss, in his eyes.

"What *was* the toughest part?" she asked, her words so soft that she wasn't sure he could hear her over the rain.

He did, and he answered, "The toughest part was never talking about it, about her, or losing her." He took a breath, let it out. "We didn't have the same type of situation that happened to Autumn, where our father dated and found someone new, and we eventually had a real family." He paused, and Maribeth wondered if he'd say something about not having church or prayer, since those were two things Autumn had mentioned, too, but he didn't. Instead, he ended with, "I'm glad Autumn had that, a real family."

"Why do you think your father didn't date or marry again? I mean, it could have been because he couldn't love anyone else," Maribeth offered, thinking that it would be amazingly romantic for a man to not be able to give his heart to another after his wife died.

Ryan laughed, but there was no humor in the sound. "You know, I think Dana may have believed that was the case for a while, that Dad couldn't love anyone but

Mom, but then I'm pretty sure she figured out the same thing I did about why he stayed single."

A shiver pulsed through her, and she wrapped the blanket around herself tighter. "And why was that?"

"Because Mom met Dad before he had anything, when he was a dirt-poor kid, raised by cotton farmers in Mississippi, who had a dream of making it big. He knew she loved him, because she'd loved him before there even was a Brooks International." He shrugged. "How would he know if someone else loved him or simply loved everything he had to offer?"

Maribeth wondered if he had any idea how much he'd just told her about himself, because she suspected she'd just learned plenty about Ryan Brooks, maybe even why someone who looked the way he looked and had everything he had was still single.

And after seeing the way he'd looked at Autumn, then watching the sweet interaction he'd had with Nathan, and now learning that there was more to Ryan Brooks than she'd realized, she suddenly had the urge to put her arm around him again, not to help him walk but to hold him close.

"Ryan," she said.

Then she remembered who he was, and that his world was different than her own, and if she were to comfort him, if she were to get that close to him... her past might resurface simply because of their association.

He looked a little uncomfortable when his eyes met hers and he apparently realized that she'd leaned toward him as she spoke. He cleared his throat. "Okay, now it's time to talk about what I wanted to discuss," he said, back to business as usual and as though he hadn't opened up to her at all.

Another flash of lightning doused the sky with white, and then gray took over again, almost as quickly as Ryan's wall had closed once more. But Maribeth had seen beneath his tough veneer, if only for a moment, and it probably wasn't a good thing that she liked— really liked—what she'd seen.

"What did you want to discuss?" she asked.

"Consigning Women," he said, "and the opportunity that you'll be losing if you don't consider letting me help you take it to the next level. You've got something that's hard to find nowadays—a unique idea and marketable concept. More than that, you have someone with the funds to take that concept and expand it to its ultimate potential."

Maribeth stopped rocking, her back straightening in the chair as she prepared to tell him—again—that she wasn't interested. And now she knew it'd be easy to maintain her emotional distance; he wasn't interested in getting closer to her. He only wanted to get control of her business.

"Consigning Women is everything I want it to be already. It has achieved its potential, as far as I want it to go." Letting him expand her business would only put Maribeth in the spotlight, as would any kind of closer relationship with Dana's brother. After the mess seven years ago, she liked where she'd landed: off the tabloid radar. And she planned to stay there.

"But why wouldn't you want to go bigger?" He frowned. "What is it *you're* not telling me? You have to see the potential here. Your dream could be huge, and you could make a difference, not only in making a name for yourself but also in helping others. Think of how many people would be able to dress the way they want, look the way they want, if you let me take your business to the next level," he said as headlights appeared on the driveway and Landon's truck started toward his and Georgiana's cabin. Maribeth knew John and Dana wouldn't be far behind.

She couldn't deny the truth. "I wouldn't mind going bigger if I knew—" she started, but then didn't know how to complete the sentence without revealing too much. She had actually thought about the possibility of owning more stores one day, but the thought of getting bigger, especially to the magnitude that she could achieve with Brooks International on board, would only serve to bring Maribeth into the public eye. Again.

"Knew what?" he asked. "Tell me, Maribeth."

"I've told you everything there is to tell," she said. Or rather, everything she was willing to share. She'd gone seven years without discussing the mistakes she'd made when she was nineteen. Her store gave her the ability to support herself and maintain her anonymity. She liked it that way, and she wasn't about to let Ryan Brooks or anyone else ruin that.

"Do you realize the amount of money you could make if you let Brooks International back you? You could go national, or even global. It'd be huge. You'd be set for life. No worries. Isn't that what everyone wants?"

"No, it isn't," she said. The only reason she'd want to grow her business would be to have the opportunity to help more people, not to grow her bank account. But she couldn't do either, because bigger meant more exposure. And she'd already been exposed enough for a lifetime.

A horn sounded as Landon, Georgiana and Abi clambered out of the truck and ran toward their cabin. Maribeth put her hand up in a wave but didn't manage a smile. She was too angry.

"Some people would rather make a difference in the world than have lots of money. Have you ever thought about that?"

"That's why you aren't growing your business? Because you want to make a difference?" he asked. "Who says you can't do both? You could make a difference *and* have plenty of income. You can't do either with your small store now."

"I *am* making a difference with my store in the square. Right now, for example, I'm pairing Nadia Berry's jewelry with outfits at the store. All proceeds from her jewelry sales go toward helping an organization that is working to stop the sex slave industry in Thailand, the country Nadia was adopted from."

He didn't miss a beat. "Think of how much more of a difference you'd make if you had more stores. You could sell that many more pieces of jewelry and *really* make a difference," he said, and Maribeth realized this man was no stranger to making his point and winning an argument, two aspects that were admittedly her weaknesses.

She regrouped. "Okay, so you've obviously got a lot of money at your disposal where you could have an impact on the world. Tell me how *you* do it."

He looked genuinely confused. "How I do what?"

"Make a difference. Because if I ever did decide to do business with someone or let someone have access to my business in any way, I'd have to know they also wanted to have a positive effect on the world." She felt her pulse pick up. She had him now, because his love of money was no secret, and she suspected he probably didn't do a thing toward making a difference in anything but his bank account. Which was a shame, since she'd seen that he could be a compassionate person when he'd talked about Autumn.

For a moment she thought he'd declare defeat, and she released the edges of the blanket and prepared to go. But then he pointed toward her and said, "Brooks International donates to several charities on a regular basis. And I've even spoken at a few of their fund-raising dinners and presented substantial checks every time. We're all about giving back."

"Tell me about one of them," she said.

"About one of the dinners?" he asked, but she suspected he knew that wasn't what she wanted to know.

"No, about one of the charities. What it stands for, why it means so much to you and why you donated toward the fund-raising."

The look of discomfort lasted less than a second, but she saw it. She had him now.

Another set of headlights shone from the driveway, and she knew John and Dana would be here soon. "You don't have to tell me about all of them," she said. "Just pick one."

He glanced at the headlights. "I have someone, actually an entire committee, that decides where the money goes."

"That's nice," she said. "That way you can give to something, even get a tax write-off, without getting emotionally involved. That's not the kind of business

I'd want to run," she said, standing and dropping the blanket to the rocker. "And it isn't the kind of business I'd want to work with. So, thanks for the offer, but I'm happy with the way things are."

Dana and John got out of their car and dashed toward the porch in the rain. "Hey," Dana said. "How was your—oh, wow, what happened?" She pointed to Ryan. "You're all muddy."

"You look like you got bucked again," John said, grinning. "And for that matter, Maribeth, so do you."

She scanned her clothes, which weren't as wet as they had been, but she'd accumulated quite a bit of the mud from Ryan when she'd helped him to the porch. She also had mud caked along the bottom third of her jeans from where she'd hit those puddles.

"I didn't get bucked," Ryan said. "But I did get thrown from my crutches. Or one of them."

"He came out to the barn for the Bible study," Maribeth explained, "and then he slid on a patch of mud on his way back to the house and one of his crutches broke."

"You went to the barn for the Bible study?" Dana's smile stretched wide. "How did you like it?"

"It was good," he said, seeming to analyze Maribeth as he spoke.

The fact that he didn't reveal his real motive for going to the barn, which she now knew had been to talk her into letting him in on her business, exasperated her, and she decided that if he was going to play that game, then so could she. "Yeah," she said, "he really liked it. And I was thinking that if he liked the Bible study so much, he'd probably enjoy church on Sunday, too."

Dana beamed. "Oh, Maribeth, that's a great idea!

Ryan, that'd be wonderful." Then she hugged John, kissed his cheek and led him into the cabin.

A moment passed after the door closed, and Maribeth felt the heat of his glare before she looked at him to verify the fact. "I've gotta go," she said.

"I never said anything about going to church." His words were clipped with barely contained frustration.

"Oh, I know," she said, "but do you know what I realized when you were comparing Autumn's story— her storm—to yours?"

"No, what?"

"That it wasn't just your father not dating or marrying that was different than Autumn's situation. She said her family started praying and going to church again. In other words, they found God, and *that* was when her storm passed." The rain let up for a moment, and Maribeth took advantage of the brief reprieve to leave the porch and start toward her car. "Good night, Ryan," she called, ready to end this emotional day.

"My storm *has* passed," he said, loud enough for her to hear before she closed the car door.

She glanced in her rearview mirror as she drove away. Another bright flash of lightning lit the sky and she saw him, the man who claimed everyone's goal had to do with money, sitting rigid on the porch, the rocker unmoving.

"Your storm hasn't passed," she said.

It didn't matter that he couldn't hear her words. She knew he wouldn't listen if he could.

Chapter Five

Ryan entertained the thought of going to church with John and Dana for a second or two when he woke Sunday morning. Then he smelled the coffee. Literally and figuratively. Pouring a cup and sipping the strong liquid—black, of course, because sugar and cream weakened the impact, and Brooks men did not like anything weak (a famous and often-repeated Lawrence Brooks quote)—Ryan focused on what he'd learned from Maribeth Walton. And it wasn't that he needed to go to church this morning.

What he needed was to make a difference in the world via Brooks International. That was the key to everything Maribeth had said Friday. Even in the charities that his company supported, Ryan had fallen into step with his father's previous contributions. It had stunned him, when Maribeth asked him to name one, that he couldn't think of any. He'd thought about the American Cancer Society shortly after she left, but he only knew that one because he'd spoken at their national fund-raiser two months ago. Since his father had been such a prominent business figure and died of the disease, the charity thought they should honor Lawrence Brooks and draw attention to their cause by having his son speak.

Ryan had enjoyed the opportunity, but even that charity was one his father had selected years ago, well before he had been diagnosed. Ryan hadn't done a thing personally to show Brooks International as a philanthropic organization, and nowadays that was an important marketing tool. People wanted to know that a company cared, and Ryan wanted it to be known that he cared, and not just about what his father had supported.

Dana entered the kitchen ready for church in the yellow dress she'd purchased from Consigning Women and holding a half-empty sleeve of saltine crackers. "Hey," she said, popping a cracker in her mouth and forcing a smile.

"Morning sickness again?" he asked.

She chewed then placed her hand against her throat as she swallowed. "They should call it all-day sickness."

He grinned. She was enjoying the pregnancy, even if the baby got the best of her most days. And she looked very pretty pregnant. She still wasn't showing, but there was something different about her; he supposed that was what they called a pregnancy glow, a happiness and excited aspect that hovered beneath the surface. "Coffee?" he asked, reaching for another mug.

Her face squished into an *ew* expression. "The thought of coffee…" She shook her head and moved her hand to her mouth.

"Okay. Think of something else. Something bland. Crackers."

She lowered her hand and laughed. "You're hysterical."

He took another sip of coffee. "Not something I hear very often, but okay."

She sat at the table and pulled another cracker from the sleeve. "I imagine you were pretty funny Friday when your crutches went sliding out from underneath you. Maribeth probably got a good laugh out of that."

He remembered Maribeth running from her car in the rain and kneeling beside him, and he also vaguely recalled that apple-and-cinnamon scent when she'd been so near. He'd liked being that close to Maribeth, even if she had taken a stubborn turn when he'd started talking business. "She didn't laugh at all. She seemed more concerned that I was okay." He smirked. "But I'm guessing that means if you'd have been the one who saw me, we'd still be out there, because you'd still be laughing."

She giggled. "You're right. But I would have made sure you were okay first, like she did, and then I would have laughed."

"Thanks." He really was enjoying this time with Dana. It'd been years since they'd had conversations that didn't involve their father or the business.

"You're welcome." She saluted him with a cracker, then popped it in her mouth.

"I talked to her about her business before she left." He didn't add that they had also talked about his mother's death, about his father's reason for staying single and about the fact that Ryan, thus far, hadn't used his resources to make a difference in the world.

Dana heaved a sigh then looked pointedly at him. "Maribeth would be good for you, Ryan."

He poured another cup of coffee. "I'm looking for a solid investment," he said. "I'm not looking for anyone to be good for me."

"Maybe you should be," she said as John came in the back door with a crutch in one hand.

"I found it over at Landon's place," he said, holding up the crutch like a prize trophy. "Broke my leg once and kept the crutches." He grinned. "I was thrown off Red, believe it or not, when he and I were a lot younger. He's not as feisty anymore, but then again, neither am I."

"I don't know about that," Dana said, and earned a wink from her husband.

"Anyway, this one may suffice, or at least hold you over until you go to rehab tomorrow and get a new one," John said. "I wanted to make sure you had it this morning since Dana said you were coming to church with us. That's great, by the way."

Ryan drank from the new cup of coffee. Hot. Strong. Perfect. "I'm not going to church," he said, "but I appreciate you going to all of the trouble. I can still use the crutch." He'd had a difficult time maneuvering around the house with just one. It was possible, but it sure wasn't easy.

John looked from Dana, now scowling at the table, to Ryan and said, "Okay. I'm gonna get a shower before we leave." He disappeared up the stairs while Ryan waited for his sister's disapproval.

She didn't keep him waiting long. "I thought you were going to church. Isn't that what you said the other night?"

"No, it was what Maribeth said," he reminded her.

"You enjoyed the Bible study. You said so."

"I did enjoy it, but I've scheduled a conference call this morning with Oliver James and expect it to take a while."

"You were on the computer and involved with conference calls all day yesterday," Dana said.

Ryan nodded. It was the truth. With the help of his public responsibilities committee, he'd meticulously studied each of the charities Brooks International supported and could now, if ever asked again, give an informed decision about how his company was making a difference. More than that, he'd realized that, given their resources, Brooks International wasn't doing nearly enough philanthropy. He planned to change that, and in doing so, put his own stamp on something that made a difference.

"We made a lot of progress yesterday in what I'm currently working on, but Oliver and I still need to discuss details for how we're moving forward." He sat across the table from his sister. "You'll be happy to know I'm working on increasing the charities the company supports. And as head of the Public Responsibilities committee, Oliver needs to be on board and support my decisions."

"I think giving more charitable donations is a great idea," she said, "but it was bad enough to make them all work on a Saturday. Now you're making Oliver work on a Sunday. He's got a new baby, if I remember right, and I'm sure he counts on his weekends for family time. Or church time, for that matter."

"If there's work to be done, you do it," Ryan said.

She gritted her teeth. "I wish you could forget all of those things Daddy used to say. And I don't care if you are working on something as positive as charities. I know that work can keep until tomorrow."

Ryan drank his coffee. Yeah, it could keep until tomorrow, but he'd been perturbed when Maribeth doled out a question about his business and he didn't have an answer. And he'd made up his mind that when he saw the feisty woman again, he would. If that meant that he and his committee worked through the weekend, so be it.

It'd also meant that he hadn't made any effort to see Maribeth yesterday. On the contrary, he'd stayed on the phone or computer and hadn't even acknowledged the camp going on except when Nathan Martin came to the cabin wanting to try out his crutches.

Remembering the boy, Ryan said, "If you see Nathan at church this morning, let him know I have two crutches now. I told him he could practice on them yesterday but he couldn't with one of them broken. Tell him he can come today if he wants, since John got that other crutch."

"You could tell him yourself if you went to church," Dana said, as John came downstairs in a button-down dress shirt and khakis.

"But I'm not, so I'm asking you to tell him for me," Ryan said.

Dana stood, grabbing her Bible and purse off the counter. "Fine. I'll tell him, but I wish you'd consider going to church with us while you're here." She blinked a couple of times, then rubbed her hand across her forehead. "And I wish you wouldn't make Oliver—or anyone—work on Sunday."

"Oliver understood the responsibilities when he took the job," Ryan said. "A willingness to put forth the extra effort is what makes Brooks International stand out from other organizations. Our *Fortune* 500 status is largely due to the fact that we never stop working."

John took his Bible from the counter and wrapped an arm around Dana. "Come on, Dana. We don't want to be late," he said, steering her toward the door.

"It's the reason we're so well-known, Dana," Ryan said, wanting her to understand. She was a Brooks, too, after all. "I learned yesterday that I was named one of *Forbes* magazine's top thirty in real estate. That doesn't come to someone who isn't willing to work weekends."

She frowned. "Congratulations, Ryan. But there's no reason you need to work this morning. I'm just afraid that you've got your priorities out of order." She shrugged. "But I still love you."

He gave her a smile. "I appreciate that. I still love you, too."

She and John left, and Ryan returned to his notes to prepare for his discussion with Oliver James. His priorities were fine. He was increasing his company's charitable contributions. What could be wrong with that?

Maribeth was so busy with the camp on Monday that she hardly had time to think about the fact that Ryan hadn't emerged from the house during last week's camp finale on Saturday, that he hadn't made an appearance at church yesterday or that he hadn't been at the window or on the porch today.

Yeah, right.

She hadn't stopped thinking about him since their conversation Friday night when, based on his disappearance ever since, it seemed he'd decided he'd had enough of Maribeth. She should be ecstatic, thrilled that he'd decided to leave her alone. And she was mad at herself that she felt anything but. Even now, standing outside of the barn as she waited for all of the parents to pick their kids up from the first camp day, she continually glanced toward John and Dana's cabin for a glimpse of the man.

But when the cabin door opened, it was Dana, not Ryan, who stepped out and started walking toward the barn.

"Maribeth, is Nadia still here? I didn't see her car," she said as she neared.

"She rode with Jasmine Waddell. That's Jasmine's car near the fence. I think they're in the tack room."

"Great. Thanks." She disappeared into the barn and emerged a few minutes later with Nadia at her side. They walked toward the cabin chatting while Maribeth answered a parent's question about her son missing a day of camp.

"Can you believe it?" Jasmine said breathlessly as she exited the barn. "Ryan Brooks wants to talk to Nadia about something. Do you think he's, like, crushing on her maybe?" She frowned. "I'd really hoped I'd get to talk to him this week and, well, maybe…"

"I don't think that's it," Maribeth said.

"I don't know. She's beautiful, with that dark hair and her unique features and everything. Maybe that's the type of look he likes."

Maribeth turned toward the girl and contemplated whether it'd control her infatuation if she told her about her past. But she suspected telling Jasmine would lead to Jasmine confiding in a few friends, and then those friends telling a few friends…

She changed tactics. "I would hope that he wouldn't

like someone merely based on appearance," Maribeth said. Truthfully, Jasmine had the look that Maribeth thought most men preferred. A lean but curvy Barbie-doll type, with long silky blond hair, big blue eyes, a full mouth. Growing up, Maribeth had wanted to look like that, but she'd learned that she didn't need to look or act a certain way to be content.

"Why do *you* think he wanted to talk to Nadia?" Jasmine asked.

"I don't know," Maribeth said, waving to the last two little girls leaving with their mom in a white mini-van and then noticing that Nadia had left the cabin and was hurrying toward them.

"Hey, there she is," Jasmine said. "Nadia! What did he want?"

Tears dripped down Nadia's cheeks, but there was no doubt that they were happy tears, because she couldn't stop smiling.

"I can't believe it," she said, looking back toward the cabin as though she expected everything to disappear in a dream.

"What? Tell us!" Jasmine demanded.

Nadia swiped at her cheeks and said, "Mr. Brooks. He told me that he knew about my ministry and how I'm trying to raise money for the women in Thailand with my jewelry sales. He said you told him about it," she said to Maribeth.

"I did. I told him about selling your jewelry at my shop," she said. She didn't add that she'd told him in order to show him what he should be doing with his own business. "What did he say about your ministry?"

"He said he's been looking into the charities that his company supports this weekend and that he's decided to add mine to the list." She giggled, her hand patting her chest as though she could feel her heart beating. "And then…then he said that he wanted to give an initial investment, money that would go directly to the shelter where I send the jewelry proceeds. Because of Mr. Brooks, once his board approves the recommendations, the Women's Lighthouse will receive a check for twenty thousand dollars. And he thinks they'll get it as quick as this week!"

"Oh, my," Maribeth whispered. Nadia had started the charity on her own after visiting her native country with her grandparents a year ago and learning about how sex slavery had affected Thailand. She had been able to send a few hundred dollars to the charity, a shelter that ran out of a church that her grandfather had started in Thailand. With Ryan's contribution and with him adding her charity to the ones Brooks International supported, Nadia had the opportunity to make a huge difference in the country.

Ryan's words from Friday night whispered through Maribeth's thoughts.

"Think of how much more of a difference you'd make if you had more stores. You could sell that many more pieces of jewelry and really make a difference."

Maribeth cringed. She *could* make a bigger difference, help more people the way Nadia was helping more, if she had additional stores. But because of her past, and her need to keep it hidden, she would forever be limited to what kind of difference she could make.

Would that mistake haunt her forever?

"Nadia, that's so incredible!" Jasmine said, and Maribeth nodded, determined to be happy for the teen.

"I know," Nadia said, bobbing her head in agreement. "It's amazing. And he's giving me ten thousand dollars to order more supplies and he's going to help me advertise. He also had an idea about people signing up for monthly donations where they would give regularly through a website."

"Without selling the jewelry to them?" Jasmine asked.

"He said that he was so impressed with the shelter and everything that they are doing that he gave money without receiving the jewelry. He believes other people will, too."

"How did he even know what the shelter was doing?" Jasmine asked.

Nadia pointed to Maribeth. "Maribeth told him about it, and then he said he was able to look at pictures of my jewelry and also found a link to information about the shelter on the Consigning Women Facebook page. Thanks so much for putting that up on your page, Maribeth."

Maribeth's emotions were in such a frenzy that her throat was dry. She forced a swallow. "I try to keep the page updated for my customers. I wanted them to know about the jewelry and the shelter at the church."

"He's so—" Jasmine sighed loudly "—incredible."

Nadia beamed. "I think so, too!" But her praise didn't sound nearly as smitten as Jasmine's. "He's been working on the details all weekend, because he had to get it approved by a committee or something. Can you believe he got it done so quickly? Isn't that wonderful?"

Maribeth nodded. "Yes, it is." Then she looked toward the cabin and wondered why Ryan had searched for the information online instead of simply asking her about the charity. She was the one who'd told him about it, after all.

Was he that irritated with her after their conversation Friday that he didn't even want to speak to her? Because she'd only been trying to help, and apparently she'd done some good. He was now contributing to a charity that she believed in. She should be content with that, instead of disconcerted that he didn't want to talk to her—and apparently even see her—anymore.

"I can't wait to tell my folks and grandparents that Mr. Brooks is helping," Nadia said. "You want to come with me, Jasmine?"

"Actually, you'll be coming with me," Jasmine said, "since I drove."

Both girls laughed as they walked toward Jasmine's car.

"See you tomorrow, Maribeth," Jasmine said, tossing her hair over her shoulder as she climbed behind the wheel.

"And thanks again for telling him about my ministry," Nadia called from the open window on the passenger side. Then she waved as they disappeared down the driveway.

Maribeth started to go to the cabin and ask Ryan why he'd left her out of his good deed. But then again, she didn't want to seem as though she wanted any credit for giving him the idea; she didn't.

And as much as she hated acknowledging the truth, she knew. She didn't want to ask him anything. She simply wanted to see him.

Chapter Six

On Tuesday, Ryan went to rehab as usual and was pleased therapy seemed to be getting easier. At the appointment that followed, Dr. Aldredge agreed that he'd progressed well and even told Ryan that he could get rid of the crutches, start getting around with the unlocked cast and letting the leg bear more weight.

Ryan had promised Nathan that he would let him have the crutches when he was finished with them, so he could practice whenever he wanted. Nathan and his family had visited the ranch Sunday afternoon, and Ryan had thoroughly enjoyed seeing the kid have such a good time with basically two long sticks. Nathan's four-year-old sister, Lainey, cheered her big brother on as he perfected his technique, and their parents, Chad and Jessica, also laughed and cheered as the family made a memory together.

The scene had touched Ryan more than he'd ever admit. He'd often wanted a family like that, so easily entertained without a high-dollar price tag or elaborate event. Even his and Dana's birthday parties had been so intricately orchestrated that they'd seemed more like work than fun. Lawrence Brooks had hired the most elite party planners and not only sent out invitations to the event, but also an itinerary of available activities and meal options. One year, when Dana had been overly obsessed with animals, their father had brought in an entire zoo. Not merely a petting zoo, like they'd seen at other parties—a whole zoo, complete with lions and tigers and everything else, had been assembled on the Brooks vacation property for party guests.

No one outdid Lawrence Brooks, in business or in pleasure. But Ryan wondered if they could have found even more enjoyment and happiness from the simple things, like a pair of crutches and a farmyard, the way Nathan's family had on Sunday afternoon.

In Ryan's opinion, that was a snapshot of the ideal family. A husband and wife undeniably in love and raising their children simply. Happily. Chad and Jessica Martin had a playful, almost flirtatious manner in which they interacted, and Ryan hadn't stayed outside with them long because he felt like an intruder.

He'd returned inside and started back to work with Oliver, but hearing their laughter and cheers, he wondered what it would feel like to have a life like that. A love like that. What would it feel like to have a wife who looked at him the way Jessica looked at Chad? Or kids who were so appreciative of something so plain and ordinary?

Merely three years ago, Ryan had thought he'd found that kind of love. His heart had fallen hard for Nannette, and he'd honestly thought she'd loved him. Not his money, but him. And then reality hit with the same force as his leg hitting the ground when Onyx sent him sailing. No mercy. No chance for his heart to stay intact. It'd broken as quickly and as severely as his leg. But his leg would heal. His heart, on the other hand, had learned its lesson.

But ever since he'd arrived in Claremont, he wondered whether he truly wanted to give up on the hope of a real love, especially when he saw so many people who seemed to have gotten it right. Like Chad and Jessica Martin. Dana and John. Landon and Georgiana. However, his past experience told him he wasn't a good judge of real, and he didn't want to risk being fooled again.

Ryan had still been working when Nathan and his family finished playing on Sunday afternoon and got ready to leave. Nathan had brought the crutches to him in the cabin, and Ryan had told him that he thought he'd be finished with them in a couple of weeks. But it turned out he was done with them today.

He looked forward to sharing that news with Maribeth. Even though he purposefully hadn't seen her since Friday, he hadn't gotten her off his mind. In fact, she'd been the primary reason he'd worked so hard over the weekend to secure approval for funding Nadia Berry's ministry and also to reevaluate the charities supported by Brooks International. He could now tell her several things about each of the organizations they supported, as well as which were his favorites. Those would be the American Cancer Society, because of his father's battle with the disease, and the Women's Lighthouse, the charity Nadia started in Thailand, which protected women from the human trafficking taking place in the country. He'd never have known about the extent of Thailand's need if it hadn't been for Maribeth, and he was happy to support such a worthy cause.

More than that, the Women's Lighthouse was the first charity Brooks International would support that had been specifically selected by Ryan instead of his father.

He'd planned to tell Maribeth yesterday, but by the time he finished talking to Nadia and then had another quick conference call with the public responsibilities committee, she was gone.

In any case, he'd tell her today, and he'd also show her that he no longer needed his crutches. It shouldn't be such a big deal to tell her, since they didn't have any type of personal relationship or anything, but it was. And Ryan began to wonder if his continued interest went beyond the fact that he wanted to invest in her business. It'd felt really nice being so close to her when she helped him from his fall, and he wondered if he wasn't feeling the beginnings of his heart slipping again.

Eager to get back to the ranch and see her, he left the rehab office and started toward the hospital elevator. Anticipating that he would be at the hospital longer today for both the physical therapy and then a short visit to Dr. Aldredge, Dana had left to run some errands until he was done. If she wasn't already waiting for him in the parking lot, she'd be there soon, but Ryan went ahead and sent her a quick text to let her know he was on his way out.

The elevator doors opened, and Hannah and Autumn Graham stepped out.

"Oh, hi," Hannah said.

"Hey," he replied. And then he looked to the little girl at her side. "Hi, Autumn."

She smiled shyly. "Hi."

Hannah patted Autumn's back and said, "Honey, if

you want to go on to Daddy's office, that's fine. He's waiting for us, and I want to tell Mr. Brooks something, okay?"

Autumn nodded. "Okay. Bye, Mr. Brooks."

"Bye, Autumn," he said, and then to Hannah said, "And it's Ryan, remember?"

She laughed. "Yes. Sorry, I forgot."

They watched Autumn as she continued down the hall. She waved before entering the office two doors down from Dr. Aldredge.

"She's a precious little girl with a tender heart," Hannah said.

Ryan nodded. "I've only been around her that short time on Friday at the Bible study, but I got that impression. Her story—" he paused "—well, it meant a lot to me, since I also lost my mom very young." He cleared his throat. "You said you wanted to talk to me about something?"

She nodded. "Yes. Like I said, Autumn has a tender heart, and she often gets these—I don't know, feelings, I guess—that someone needs special prayers." A smile lifted her lips. "If she knows someone is sick, she'll pray specifically for that person until they are better again or until they go to heaven, like her mom did. She has a really big way of thinking about things like that. I suppose it's because she lost her mom when she was so young."

"That makes sense," Ryan said.

"But ever since she met you on Friday, she's been praying for you. Every time she prays, whether it's at night before bed or even before we eat, she prays for Mr. Ryan and she says she hopes he'll feel better soon."

She shrugged, while Ryan's heart tugged solidly in his chest. "I just thought I should let you know."

Ryan's throat tightened, and he cleared it before saying, "I appreciate that, and I'll need to tell her that the prayers worked. My leg is getting better, and I don't even need these anymore." He indicated his crutches.

"That's great," Hannah said, "but..." She glanced down the hall toward the door her daughter had entered.

"Is there something else?" he asked, curious.

She looked as though she debated completing the rest of the sentence and hesitated for a second before saying, "It's just that I don't think she's praying for your leg, exactly. I mean, I'm sure she wants you to heal, but her prayers are more God focused."

"God focused?" he asked.

"She's praying for you to know God." Another soft smile claimed her lips. "Like I said, she has really big ways of thinking for a child so young, and when she gets things like that on her heart, she prays."

Taken aback, Ryan didn't know what to say. That little girl was praying for him to know God? How did she know that he didn't?

As though reading his thoughts, Hannah continued, "I don't know what your spiritual life is like, Mr. Brooks—Ryan—and in case you're thinking someone has been speculating about it or talking about you like that, I want to let you know that couldn't be further from the truth. When I asked Autumn why she thought you needed to know God, she said, 'Because everyone should know Him, and because I like Mr. Ryan.'"

The elevator had closed a while back, but now the doors reopened as a man exited on their floor.

"I should head on out," Ryan said, indicating the open elevator. "Dana is probably waiting in the parking lot."

She nodded solemnly. "Okay."

He got inside the elevator. "Please thank Autumn for me. I do appreciate her prayers. I'm just—well, I'm not all that used to people praying for me."

Hannah's face instantly converted to a smile. "I will thank her," she said, as the bell dinged and the doors prepared to slide closed, "and Ryan?"

"Yes?" he asked when the doors started to move.

"I'll be praying for you, too."

Maribeth entered the feed room in the barn and found the molasses treats that she'd promised the campers they could give the horses this afternoon. With sixteen preteen kids at this week's camp, she had to make sure she stayed organized and ready for every activity. Unlike last week's campers, these kids weren't local, but were from a church in Birmingham. Because of that, Maribeth had more help than she'd anticipated. Parents didn't merely drop off their kids and pick them up at the end of the day. Instead, chaperones stayed and assisted in the activities. And at the end of the day, the kids and chaperones stayed and camped in tents on the riverbank at the base of Jasper Falls. They not only had the Bible study that Maribeth led at the end of the camp day, but they also had Bible studies by campfire at night led by John, Dana, Landon and Georgiana. Maribeth had attended summer church camps growing up, but never one like this. She and her sisters would have enjoyed the dude ranch activities, riding horses, hiking the nature trails and camping in tents.

Thoughts of her sisters reminded her of how rarely she saw them, primarily at holidays, because she didn't want to leave her business unattended. Maybe she could hire someone to allow her to get away without risking losing customers because the shop was closed. Or maybe it didn't matter if she closed the doors for a couple of days every now and then. Maribeth wasn't sure. She had Theapia Best, a responsible nineteen-year-old, working the store during the mornings this month so she could volunteer at the camp, but maybe she should hire someone more permanently. If she allowed Ryan to invest in her business and open more stores, he'd probably help her make decisions like that, or he'd hire someone to help her. She had no idea what he'd do or how he'd do it. All she knew is that he'd make her business bigger.

But she didn't necessarily want Consigning Women to be bigger. She wanted it to be successful, which it was for her current demographic. And, more important, she wanted it to make a difference.

Ryan's statement that she could make a bigger difference in the world if she had more locations was probably true. But was it worth putting her name out there and risking someone putting two and two together and then resurrecting her past? She liked the way she had disappeared into the fabric of Claremont with no limelight whatsoever on that life she'd led seven years ago. Her past was so embarrassing, such a colossal tribute to the stupidity and naivety of a teen. Her parents had warned her, and she hadn't listened. Her sisters had begged her to think about what she was doing, and she'd told them they were jealous.

So many mistakes. And her family had forgiven all

of them, as had God. Maribeth wondered whether the offer from Ryan to grow her business was a chance for her to truly make a bigger difference in the world, or whether it was the ultimate temptation to have everything that she'd had seven years ago…and everything that had been taken away.

She withdrew her cell phone from her jeans pocket and dialed her older sister's number.

"Maribeth, so good to hear from you. How's everything going?" Ava answered, obviously taking advantage of caller ID to jump right into conversation. She was always on high gear, with her two-year-old twins keeping her on her toes.

"Everything's going fine," Maribeth said.

"You're volunteering at the church camp there, aren't you? The dude ranch? Isn't that what you said you'd be doing during the day in June?"

It'd been several weeks since the two had talked, but Ava remembered what would be happening in Maribeth's world. It touched Maribeth that she cared so much. "Yes, I'm actually at the ranch now."

"I don't hear any kids."

"I'm by myself for the time being," Maribeth explained. "The group is at the Sanders farm next door practicing riding the horses in the round pen. Mrs. Sanders is Georgiana's mom, and she teaches riding lessons, so she offers a day of lessons as part of the camp. Dana's niece, Abi, demonstrates techniques for the campers, and then their lunch for today is served at the Sanders ranch." She glanced at the time on her phone. "I'll need to head back over in about an hour to take them on the afternoon trail ride before Bible study. Then some of my friends will run the evening activities so I can work at the store."

"Wow, you have a lot going on, don't you?"

"I do, but I enjoy it," Maribeth said. She'd never been one to appreciate idle time and liked being busy.

Ava sighed. "Oh, Maribeth, I'm glad everything has worked out so well for you there. I can tell by the way you talk about everyone that they're almost like family. It's just that I still wish you would move back here and be with all of us again."

This was an ongoing request from Ava, their younger sister, Deidre, and their parents, but as much as she missed her family, Maribeth didn't have any desire to move back to the beach. Too many painful memories. "I know, but I don't think I will be coming back for more than visits. This is my home now, and you're right that many people here are almost like family to me." She paused, then added, "Though no one can take your place."

Ava chuckled. "Oh, I know that. I—hang on." Apparently covering the phone with her hand, she said, "Libby, aren't you supposed to be resting?"

"Sarah is playing." Libby's voice was soft, but even muffled by Ava's hand over the receiver, Maribeth could tell she was tattling.

Maribeth listened as Ava told both of the girls to climb back on their respective beds and rest. A tiny chorus of *yes, ma'am*s followed, and then Ava returned to the line. "Sorry about that. Now what were we saying?"

"That no one could take my family's place?" Maribeth answered.

Ava laughed. "That's right, and it's true. But what I

planned to ask was whether you'd met anybody there that didn't seem like family? Like, maybe even more special than your fabulous family?"

Maribeth smiled. "No," she answered, the way she always did when Ava or Deidre or their mother posed the love-interest question. And then, for some reason, she added, "Not really."

Ava jumped all over the extra tidbit with fervor. "Not really? Wait a minute. What does that mean?"

"Nothing. I don't know why I said that," Maribeth said, and winced at the lie.

"Yes, you do, and I'm not getting off this phone until you tell me. What's his name? And do you think he might be the one? Is he from Claremont? Will he love your family? And, biggest question here, how is his relationship with God?"

Maribeth decided to start with the easiest of the questions. "Any guy would love all of you, no doubt."

"Yeah, that's true, but what about the rest?" Ava asked.

Maribeth loved Ava's interpretation of their family, and the yearning in her heart got a little stronger at the realization that they were fabulous and she'd turned her back on them way back when. But she wouldn't turn her back on them again, and her sister had asked her questions and wanted answers. Maribeth would give them to her.

"I have only talked to him. We haven't been out on a date or anything like that, and I don't even think he's interested. Matter of fact, I'm pretty sure I ticked him off enough that he may never want to see me again. So to say whether he is the one would be extremely premature."

Ava giggled into the phone. "What did you do to tick him off?"

"I'm pretty sure it was when I told him he wasn't trying to make a difference in the world and that he should. Or maybe it was when I tried to manipulate him into going to church on Sunday. Or it could have been…"

Ava's giggle turned to full-blown laughter. "Oh, Maribeth, you have a funny way of showing someone that you like them."

"I didn't say I liked him."

"Yeah, I think you did," she said, finally gaining control of herself. "And—wait a minute—you said you tried to manipulate him into going to church? So, he isn't on great terms with the big guy?"

Maribeth admired her sister's relationship with her heavenly father and the fact that she saw Him not only as her father but also as her friend. Her comfortable term for Him didn't bother Maribeth; on the contrary, it reminded her of the relationship that He offered. He was what each of His children needed, a father and a friend.

"Ryan hasn't had an opportunity to learn a lot about God," she said, and then she realized that probably wasn't true. "Or he hasn't taken an opportunity to learn," she said. "I know Dana has tried to talk to him and get him to think about his faith, but I think he may have some issues there." She thought about their conversation on the porch Friday night. "May even blame God for the fact that he lost his mother when he was young and then that his family situation wasn't exactly the norm."

Silence echoed through the line.

Maribeth waited a beat and then asked, "Ava? You still there?"

"I am. I'm just in shock at what I *think* you're telling me."

"That he isn't close to God? There are a lot of people who aren't, and that doesn't mean they can't grow spiritually. I mean, just look at where I was right after I left home. But I came back to my faith." If anyone knew how being apart from God could make you even closer when you returned to Him, it was Maribeth.

"That's not what shocks me. What shocks me is the name you tossed out as though it's no big deal. You said Ryan. And then you said that Dana has been trying to talk to him about his faith. The only Dana you ever talk about is Dana Cutter, formerly Dana Brooks. And if she's talking to this Ryan about his faith, I'm assuming that you're referring to her brother, Ryan Brooks. Is *that* who you're talking about, Maribeth?"

Maribeth peeked out of the tack room to make sure no one had entered the barn and was privy to this conversation. The place was blessedly empty. "Yes. Ryan Brooks," she said.

"Maribeth. Oh, my. I—I don't know what to say. This is so similar to—" She paused. "I mean, he's rich. He's drop-dead gorgeous. He can have his pick of probably any single woman in the world. He isn't all that keen on his spirituality."

"Yet," Maribeth interjected, because, in spite of the fact that they probably weren't even on speaking terms now, she still felt that God had put Ryan in her life so she could help him with his faith. But Ava was undoubtedly thinking the same thing that had crossed Maribeth's mind about a relationship with a guy like

Ryan Brooks. He was eerily similar to the one man she'd trusted before, and merely being seen with him could put her back in the limelight again. And could therefore cause the media to dig into her past.

Being with Ryan Brooks could make her front-page news. Again. That had nearly destroyed her before and should be enough reason to cause her to steer away from Ryan completely.

So why couldn't she stop thinking about him, even now, when Ava was reminding her of the last time she gave her heart to a rich boy?

"Okay, I'll give him the benefit of the doubt there, because people can change when it comes to their faith," Ava said. "But even that notwithstanding, all of those things make him…exactly what you had before."

She should've known her sister's thoughts had followed the same path as her own. Ava knew how terribly Maribeth had been hurt before. "I know." Those facts had been plaguing Maribeth all week, ever since she'd realized that she simply wasn't content on the days she didn't get to see Ryan.

"Oh, Maribeth. I hear it in your voice. You're falling in love with him, aren't you?" Ava asked, never one to hold back.

Even the possibility that she might be falling in love with Ryan was like a kick in the stomach. She should know better. But maybe she didn't even need to worry about it. Chances were, he'd already decided not to talk to her again. "Like I said, I ticked him off, so we're not even speaking, best I can tell. Kind of hard to love someone who isn't talking to you."

"No, it isn't, but I'll give you a pass and wait until you're ready to admit it. I *can* hear it in your voice already, though. It reminds me so much of that day when you came home from the beach after seeing—"

"Don't say it," Maribeth pleaded. Those memories haunted her on a daily basis, and she didn't need Ava making them any more vivid.

"Okay. Just remember that you can call me about anything. And I can be there in five hours. Mom can watch the girls, or Michael can take off work and stay home with them. What I'm trying to say is I'm here for you, and I can be there for you if you need me. I don't want to see you hurt again. And I *refuse* to let anyone break your spirit again." The last sentence was spoken with so much conviction that tears pushed free from Maribeth's eyes and trickled down her cheeks. Ava was so protective of her, and she appreciated that protection deeply. "I love you, sis," Ava said.

"I love you, too," Maribeth said. "I'll keep you posted on whatever happens here."

"Call me if you need me, and remember that I'm praying for you. We all pray for you."

"I pway for Em-beth."

"Sarah, you're supposed to be resting," Ava said.

"I pway for Em-beth," the little girl repeated, loud enough for Maribeth to hear and for fresh tears to leak free.

"Tell her I said thank you for the prayers," Maribeth said.

"I'll tell her. Call me back tomorrow and let me know what's happening there."

Typically they talked once a week, but Maribeth knew that if she didn't call Ava tomorrow then her sister would be calling her. Ava was ready to watch over her as she waded back into the waters of potential love, and she appreciated her thoughtfulness. "I'll call," she promised.

They disconnected and Maribeth sat on a stack of saddle blankets, wiped her eyes and silently prayed. *God, You know Ava is right. If I let my heart keep falling for Ryan, because I do think it's falling, then I'm following the same pattern as before. I promised myself and You that I'd never let that happen again. And I prayed for You to get Ryan back to Chicago. Obviously, You said no to that request. Why, Lord? Is it because this time it's different? He's different? Or is it because I'm supposed to resist the temptation to make the same mistakes again?*

Tears fell, and she let them. Her emotions were in a frenzy, and she needed help. *Show me the answer here, Lord. Help me to make a wise decision in how I handle this infatuation with Ryan. And if there is the potential for love, real love, then let me know that, too, God. I love You and I praise You. In Your son's holy name, amen.*

Maribeth opened her eyes and immediately heard someone in the barn. She was certain anyone who saw her now would be able to tell she'd been crying, and she didn't want to try to explain her tears, so she sat quietly and said another silent prayer that the person would be on their way soon. She only had half an hour before she was supposed to meet the kids at the Sanders farm.

A soft humming accompanied the person on the other side of the wall and Maribeth thought she remembered Jasmine humming the same tune earlier today. She had been at the Sanders farm with the others when Maribeth came back to get the molasses treats. Jasmine was doing a great job helping with the kids, even if she did spend a lot of her time looking for and talking about Ryan. So far, to her dismay, he'd yet to make an appearance this week.

And to Maribeth's dismay, too.

A deep clearing of a throat alerted Jasmine—and Maribeth—that a man had now entered the barn. Even with the occasional gap in the wooden planks forming the tack room walls, Maribeth couldn't see who the guy was, but from Jasmine's reaction, she suspected that she knew.

"Oh, wow, um, hi," Jasmine said, her voice practically dripping with flirtation.

"Hello." Ryan's voice, as deep and rich as always, sent a shiver down Maribeth's spine.

"I'm Jasmine. I'm helping with the church camp this week."

"Nice to meet you, Jasmine."

"Um, well, did you need something in the barn? Can I help you with anything?"

"I was looking for someone," he said, "but I can come see her later. I've got work to do anyway."

"Wait!" Jasmine sounded panicked that he'd finally shown up and was leaving.

"Yes?"

"Maybe I can help you. Who are you looking for?"

"Maribeth Walton," he said, and Maribeth's skin tingled merely from hearing him say her name. Ava was right. She was falling. Hard.

"Maribeth?" Jasmine questioned. "Are you two, you know, dating or something?"

"No."

The single word stabbed Maribeth in the heart.

"Oh, okay then," Jasmine said, her tone happy again. "I'll tell her that you're looking for her."

"I would appreciate that," he said.

"So…" Jasmine said, and she seemed to be moving toward the other side of the barn, where Ryan apparently stood, "*are* you dating anyone?" A nervous giggle trickled after the last word.

Maribeth's stomach pitched, not because Jasmine was so blatantly making a move on Ryan, but because she remembered asking a similar question once upon a time, and she remembered how that had turned out.

Would Ryan also take advantage of a young girl's infatuation? Would he lead her on until he got what he wanted, and then drop her when he wanted something else? Would he make her betray her faith? Would he cause her to leave her family? Would he change her life forever, the way Maribeth's life had been changed back then?

"Jasmine—" his deep voice echoed through the barn and settled against Maribeth's chest "—you seem like a very sweet girl…"

"I'm nineteen," she said, "definitely not a girl."

Maribeth could tell by the way her words got softer that she was still moving toward the other side of the barn, toward Ryan.

"And everyone says I'm mature for my age," she added. "I was just thinking that if you weren't dating anyone—because I wouldn't want anyone to get upset with me or anything—but if you aren't, then maybe while you are in Claremont, I could, you know, show you around or something."

"Jasmine," he said, and there was a long pause that made Maribeth wonder if he were about to do something dramatic, like kiss her, because she knew what that was like, too, for the guy to give you hope that this was happily ever after and for you to believe it because you want to. "I've just met you," Ryan continued, "and like I said, you seem like a sweet girl."

"If you think I'm too young for you to date…" she started, but Ryan halted her.

"The thing is, you need to know someone, connect with them and care about them, if you want to have a relationship with them. And you deserve to have someone that knows you, cares about you and respects you as a person to date."

"You go out with different girls all the time," she said. "I've seen the pictures in the magazines and on the internet. And it looks like you normally only go out with them once, except for that Nannette girl that married the baseball player. I remember that one time when one of those magazines said you had secretly married her, or you were trying to plan a secret wedding or something like that." She paused, apparently waiting for Ryan to say something. When he didn't, she barreled on. "So go out with me one time and see if you might want to go out again. Maybe it's the city girls that you don't like. Maybe you need someone who, you know, likes the simple things?"

"Jasmine, listen, please. I'm not trying to hurt you, and I want to make sure you understand. First of all, as far as those pictures are concerned, most of those women were one-time dates because I knew that I didn't want a relationship with any of them and that they weren't interested in a relationship, either. We attended events together because there were no strings.

If any of them had wanted something long-term, I wouldn't have asked them out."

"Well, this wouldn't even really be a date. I'd like to show you around Claremont," she said, hope still evident in her tone. "That's all."

Ryan's deep sigh was loud enough that Maribeth heard it.

"Jasmine," he said, "you are a beautiful girl—young lady—and I'm going to tell you the truth. You're selling yourself short here. You don't know me."

"But—" she started.

"You may have read about me in the tabloids and online, but that isn't the same as knowing someone. Many times the things they publish aren't even true or may be partial truths. And I get that you want to show me around town, but I also feel that you may be expecting that tour to turn into something more, and it won't."

Jasmine gasped, and Maribeth put her hand to her mouth. The blankets shifted beneath her with the movement, and she held her breath and braced for someone to open the door.

A moment passed, and she released the breath and strained her ears to see if Ryan would say more. She didn't want him to lead Jasmine on, but she didn't want him to be cruel, either.

He must have taken a moment to think about his words, because another beat passed before he continued.

"The reason it won't," he said, "is because you deserve someone who wants to go out with you because they have feelings for you, someone that knows you and the type of person you are, someone that you can connect with emotionally and someone who you can give your heart to." There was a brief pause, and then he added, "And someone who will give his heart to you. You deserve more than I could give."

Jasmine sniffed loudly. "I—I'm so embarrassed. I mean, how stupid, to think someone like you would even be the least bit interested—"

"That's not it," he said. "I told you the truth. You are beautiful and intriguing, and if I were a different kind of man, I would take you up on that tour and maybe see what would come after. But it wouldn't be what you want, and it isn't what I want, either, not because I wouldn't be interested in you, but because I won't let myself take advantage of you. There's a guy out there who will give you that long-term love that you want, and I want to make sure you aren't wasting your feelings on me."

Another uncomfortable pause magnified the creaks and echoes that were typical in the barn, then Jasmine sniffed loudly once more. "Are you going to tell anyone, like Dana, about this?" Jasmine asked.

"No," he said, and when she sniffed again, he added, "you have my word."

"I'm a fool, aren't I?"

He laughed softly. "No, you're not. You're ambitious and not afraid to go after something you want. I'm thinking that'll probably take you far in business one day, should you choose that route."

Another loud sniffle, and then Jasmine cleared her throat. "I want to own a shop in the square one day. I don't know what kind yet, but that's what I want to do, the way Maribeth owns her place."

"That's a great goal," he said. "And if you have any

questions about starting your business at that time, you know you can ask me."

"Thanks," she said, still sniffing but sounding a little more normal. "And thanks for not telling Dana or anyone about me, you know, kind of hitting on you, or whatever you call it." She laughed.

"You're welcome."

"Hey, you said you were looking for Maribeth. Do you want me to tell her when I see her?"

"No, I'll find her later, but thanks for offering."

Maribeth listened as Jasmine apparently moved toward the tack room, and she said another quick prayer that the girl wouldn't open this door and find her eavesdropping on their private conversation. She hadn't meant to; she'd simply not wanted to come out and let anyone see that she'd been crying.

Thankfully, Jasmine moved past the tack room, but then she stopped and called out, "Ryan?"

"Yeah?"

"I was just thinking that Maribeth doesn't date anyone, and she's older, you know, like more your age."

His laugh filled the air. "So now I'm older? Is that it?"

"No, that isn't what I meant. I was just, you know, thinking about the fact that you were looking for her and then I got to thinking that maybe if you met someone like Maribeth, someone who you already know and someone who is like you, kinda, then maybe you should ask her out and see if she's a more-than-one-date type girl for you."

"Someone like me?" he asked.

"She started her own business, and it's doing really good, I think. I know it's not as big and everything like yours, but it's a pretty big deal for Claremont. And, well, we all like her, but she's never really dated anyone. I was just thinking that she should have someone cool in her life, and you need to date someone more than once sometime."

"I do?" Humor laced the question.

"Yeah," she said, undeterred. "Because, well, you're like, what? Thirty, right?"

"Thirty-one next month," he said.

"So, you were already pushing the limit for me," she said. "But you'd be good for Maribeth, and pretty soon, you know, you'll be considered too old, I mean, for some people…"

This time he didn't hold his laugh back, and it echoed against the rafters. "Jasmine, you have gone from flattering me to deflating me in the span of fifteen minutes."

She laughed. "Sorry. I just think you should think about it."

"Okay."

"Well, I've got to get back to the kids at the camp. I guess we're okay, right? I mean, if I see you around, it's fine to say hello? You won't feel funny talking to me after I acted so stupid?"

"Please say hello," he said.

"Okay. I will." Then she started walking away again and after a few seconds, Maribeth thought she heard her humming the tune from earlier.

Maribeth waited, listening for signs that Ryan had also left the barn. She didn't hear anything for a moment, and relief flooded through her…then the tack room door opened and revealed the heart-stopping presence of Ryan Brooks. But Maribeth's heart didn't stop; in fact, it pounded so powerfully that she felt each beat in her throat.

Now what would she do?

Chapter Seven

Ryan knew he'd heard something when he and Jasmine were talking. At first he'd thought it might have been one of the barn cats that often hovered in and around the stalls, but none of them made an appearance. He'd continued listening while he had the awkward conversation with Jasmine and hadn't heard the noise again, but still, he had this feeling that they were being watched, or at the very least listened to.

Opening the tack room door, he learned his gut feeling was, as usual, spot-on. "Care to let me know what you were doing in there, or why you didn't say anything when we were talking?"

Maribeth looked as striking as ever sitting on a stack of colorful saddle blankets wearing a red-and-white checked shirt, worn jeans that were frayed at the knees, a straw cowboy hat and boots. Her hair was braided and hung over her right shoulder, a bright red ribbon threaded through the dark locks. Add to all of that the cheeks that flamed due to being caught eavesdropping and her face as guilt ridden as a kid with her hand in the cookie jar, and she was downright adorable.

"I, um," she started, then her dark brows dipped and she frowned.

"Yes?" he asked, and wasn't too happy with himself that he was enjoying this.

She blinked, straightened on the blankets and seemed to gather her bearings. "I wasn't hiding in here hoping to listen to barn conversations, if that's what you think. I came in here to get molasses treats for the kids to give the horses this afternoon."

"And then you stayed in there because you heard Jasmine and me talking?"

She shook her head, and the long dark braid shifted on her shoulder. "No, I stayed in here because it was quiet, and I wanted a little privacy to..."

"To what?" he asked.

"Pray."

Okay. Not what he was expecting. "There seems to be a lot of that going around," he mumbled, remembering Hannah's statement that Autumn had been praying specifically for him.

"What?" she asked.

He shook his head. "Nothing. So you were praying and then you heard us talking, and you decided to stay quiet."

"No, not to begin with," she said. "I stayed quiet when I heard Jasmine in the barn because I didn't want to come out yet."

"You hadn't found the molasses treats?" he asked, and he zeroed in on the treats beside her on the blankets.

"No, I had found them, but I didn't want her to see me crying."

That got his attention. "I thought you said you were praying."

"I was," she said, turning away from him to retrieve a small burlap bag. She began to scoop the treats together and then put them in the bag, keeping her eyes diverted from Ryan through the process.

He knew she didn't want to look at him, but that didn't mean he was done asking her questions. "You cry when you pray?"

She slowed down placing the treats in the bag but didn't look up. "Sometimes." Then, when the last piece of molasses fell into the bag, she finally turned back to Ryan.

He waited until her eyes met his and then said, "I'm still not understanding why you didn't say something and let us know you were here."

"I don't know why I didn't," she said. "I heard the two of you start talking, and the conversation was so… sensitive…that then I didn't want you or Jasmine to know I'd heard any of it."

"But I know."

"Yeah." She grabbed the bag and stood. "Listen, I know I shouldn't have been eavesdropping, but I did, and I think you should know that it was wonderful how you handled that with Jasmine."

Ryan wasn't prepared to take a compliment for merely doing the right thing. "Okay."

She shook her head. "No, I mean it. You could have hurt her, in several ways. You could have turned her down flat and made her think she wasn't worthy of your attention. Or you could have ignored her, which would have basically left her feeling the same way." She took a deep breath, pushed it out. "Or you could have made her think you *were* interested and then you could've…you could've…" She blinked again, and to Ryan's dismay a tear dripped from each eye. She brushed them away and shook her head as though willing additional tears to stay put. "Well, I want you to know that even though I shouldn't have heard your conversation, I did, and I want to thank you for not breaking her spirit…or her heart."

"I wouldn't do that," he said softly, "to Jasmine, or to anyone else."

The blinking continued, and she visibly swallowed. "I believe you," she whispered.

"I'm glad."

Her phone started beeping, and she slid it from her jeans pocket. "I need to start the hike back if I'm going to meet up with the group when they get done at the other farm. They'll be ready for a trail ride in fifteen minutes, and I need to be there."

"Why don't you ride one of the horses?" he asked. "That'd be quicker, wouldn't it?"

She pointed out the rear of the barn and toward the lone stallion in the field. "Onyx is the only one we didn't take over for the lessons, and we both know what happens when someone tries to ride him." She glanced toward Ryan's leg. "Hey, you don't have your crutches."

"Nope. The doctor okayed me walking with the brace now, and I think I'm doing pretty good."

"Not too sore?"

"Still hurts, but nothing I can't handle."

Her phone beeped again. "I need to go."

"One more thing," he said, reaching for her forearm and then finding his hand closing gently around her skin. He liked the way it felt, and when he glanced up and saw her looking at his palm against her arm, he thought she might like it, too. "I wanted to thank you."

"Thank me?" she asked.

"For questioning me about the charities Brooks International supported and for telling me to look at what Nadia was doing with her ministry. I spent the past few days doing both, evaluating our charitable organizations and also researching the Women's Lighthouse, and I've made some changes that I feel really good about. That's because of you. So thanks."

Her mouth lifted in a smile. "Nadia told me about your generous support. She was thrilled," she said, then added, "and so was I. So I guess that's what had you so busy this weekend, too busy to visit the church?" Then, before he had a chance to answer, she continued, "Oh, I shouldn't have said that. I'm sorry. Sometimes I get a little forward in my evangelizing." Her laugh was soft and sweet, and Ryan liked it. A lot.

"Actually, it's fine for you to ask. I was busy with our public responsibilities committee, having them vet the organizations we're supporting, as well as the Women's Lighthouse, but I could've gone to church if I'd really wanted to. At the time, I didn't think I wanted to go."

"At the time?" she asked hopefully, her hands beginning to fidget with the small burlap bag. "Has that changed?"

"Apparently, several people in Claremont have been praying for me, for some reason, and I guess I feel I should do something about that."

She looked skeptical. "You shouldn't let anyone guilt you into going to church. You should go because you want to."

"I didn't mean it like that. I don't feel guilted into it, but I'm finding myself a little curious about all of this religion I'm surrounded by down here, and I'd like to see what it's all about before I head home to Chicago."

"I think that's a great idea," she said, and her phone started ringing this time. She answered, "Hey." A few nods, and then she said, "I'll meet y'all there."

"You have to go," he said.

"I do, but I've enjoyed talking to you, and I've come to realize something about you this afternoon, Ryan Brooks."

"What's that?" he asked.

"You're not all that bad."

Chapter Eight

Ryan got the approval he needed from the board to go ahead with the PR committee's recommended changes for charitable contributions, which included adding the Women's Lighthouse at the church in Thailand to the groups supported by Brooks International. In fact, the money would have already been put into the organization's account and available for helping the women in Nadia's birth country. He'd kept an eye out for the campers returning to the barn from their trail ride so he could tell Nadia, but he hadn't seen them yet.

At a little past three, he went to the barn to see if anyone was there and knew when the group would head back. His knee was still getting used to the additional weight incurred without the crutches, but even Ryan could tell that he was doing pretty well, like Dr. Aldredge had said. In fact, he wouldn't be surprised if he finished his therapy earlier than the six weeks that the doctor had anticipated.

That thought both excited him, because he'd be able to return to all of his regular physical activities and work, and disheartened him, because he'd be leaving Claremont—and a certain brunette beauty that he couldn't get off his mind. Seeing Maribeth earlier made him realize how much he'd missed her over the past few days and how much he enjoyed being around the intriguing lady. She seemed so genuine, very real in her thoughts and actions. And she didn't seem like the type that'd be able to fake those qualities.

Neither had Nannette, he realized. But Ryan had started to wonder if he wanted to give up on the prospect of love completely just because of one woman who hadn't been what she'd seemed, who'd only wanted Ryan's status and income. Maribeth certainly didn't seem to care about either of those things; she didn't even want her business to expand beyond the Claremont town limit. Wasn't that a sure sign that she didn't care about money? And when they were together, Ryan didn't think he was the only one dealing with a powerful attraction.

He'd wanted to kiss her today. The desire to hold her, protect her, was nearly overpowering. Protect her. Why did he feel that she needed protecting? She hadn't said anything, but still, Ryan could tell that she was guarded, as if she'd allow him to see the surface of her emotions but nothing more. And he wanted to know more about Maribeth.

Ryan had been watching for the group so he could tell Nadia his news, but he'd also been watching so he'd get another chance to talk to Maribeth.

"You're not all that bad."

Hardly a compliment, but coming from Maribeth, it'd made his pulse jump.

Memories of Nannette, and the way her compliments had meant the world to him because he'd thought she'd truly meant every word and didn't care about his title or his money, filled him, and he grimaced not only because of the pain in his knee but also from the smarting of her betrayal. He'd been so certain she truly cared about him. Could he trust his judgment to ever know whether a woman, like Maribeth, really did?

He reached the barn to find that the group hadn't returned from the trail ride, and only one farmhand working inside, carrying fifty-pound feed sacks from the bed of a pickup to the feed room.

The guy dropped a bag on top of his current stack and then started back toward the truck. He saw Ryan, wiped the sweat from his brow with his forearm and said, "Oh, Mr. Brooks. Hi."

"Hello," Ryan said, entering the barn. A month ago, he'd have started helping the guy out with the feed sacks, but even though he'd ditched his crutches today, he wasn't ready for hauling the fifty-pound bags.

"Heard about Onyx throwing you," he said, then pointed to Ryan's leg. "Looks like you're doing better. That's good."

"I am, and thanks."

He stuck out a hand. "I'm Cory, by the way, Cory Shields. I help out at the farm. I guess you can see that," he added with a grin. "Actually, I work at all of the farms around here. Just fill in wherever I can to keep the work steady, you know."

Ryan nodded. At first he'd thought Cory was a teen, maybe a senior baseball player or something, with his tall muscled build, but now that he was up close, he could see that Cory was older. Probably early twenties. "It's commendable to see someone that dedicated to their work," Ryan said.

Cory touched his cowboy hat and rolled his lips in as though wondering how to respond. Then he let out a low grunt and said, "I didn't exactly have the best work ethic to start with, and that's kind of why I'm working farm to farm." He shrugged. "But I learned my lesson, or that's what my dad says, and I'm trying to start over."

"That's commendable, too," Ryan said.

"You know, I've been wanting to talk to you, ask you what you think of what I'm doing, because you're so successful in business and everything, but I didn't know if you'd like people asking you questions out of the blue. I'm guessing folks probably hit you up all the time for info on how to make it in the business world, and you probably get tired of it. So I'd made up my mind to let you be and not bother you."

"Cory, if you've got a business question, I'd be happy to try to answer it," Ryan said, impressed that he'd first tried to respect Ryan's privacy and then found the courage to state what was on his mind. He took an instant liking to the young man, whom he'd personally seen working diligently at the farm nearly every day. Whether he'd had a good work ethic in the past or not, he had one now, and that's what mattered in Ryan's book.

Cory removed his work gloves and slapped them together, then tossed them on a bale of hay nearby. "Okay then. I won't waste your time, and I'll just tell you the truth. I got a scholarship fresh out of high school to play baseball for Florida State."

"Whoa," Ryan said. "That's impressive."

"Yeah, it would've been, if I'd kept myself out of the partying on campus, and if I'd opened a book every now and then to study, and if I'd shown up for more than fifty percent of my classes."

"That's the previous work ethic you're talking about," Ryan said.

"Yeah, work ethic, school ethic, whatever you call it. Basically no ethics, if you want to get right down to it. So I lost my scholarship after a year and ended up coming back home."

"Which is how you got here, working on the farm?" Ryan asked.

"Pretty much. But the thing is, once I lost everything, the scholarship and the chance to play college ball, I realized that I'd missed my chance. That was my big break, my chance to get a degree paid for by the university. My folks told me they weren't going to pay for me to go to school, because I'd had my chance. They said if I want a degree, then I've got to save and pay my own way."

"Is that what you're doing now, working all of these hours at multiple farms?"

"I've got half the money saved up so far, and if I keep working extra hours, I should have the rest by next summer, so I can start college again that fall semester."

"Again, I'm impressed," Ryan said truthfully. "But you said you had a business question for me."

Cory tilted his hat. "I do. I want you to tell me the truth. If a guy like me came in for a job interview, and you saw that he totally blew that first year of school, took another two years off to regroup and then went back and did it right, studying and hopefully acing his classes and cutting out the partying, would you hire him? Or is the fact that I've already messed up once a reason not to? I'm just wondering…am I going to still have a chance at a decent job, or have I ruined that?"

Ryan had been impressed with everything he'd seen and heard from Cory Shields already, but his honesty magnified his impression. "The way I see it, you're showing a potential employer that you don't give up when you make a mistake and that you're willing to do whatever it takes and work however hard you have to in order to make it right. I honestly do not think it will do anything to hurt you in today's job market."

"That's what I was hoping you'd say. Thanks, Mr. Brooks." The smile that claimed Cory's face made Ryan grin in return.

"You're welcome."

The sound of horses' hooves caused the two of them to turn and see three horses emerging from the wooded trails to cross the fields toward the barn. Nadia rode John's horse, Red, Jasmine rode Landon's horse, Samantha—"Sam"—and in between them, Maribeth rode Fallon. Apparently, their work day was over, and John and Dana, along with the chaperones who were spending the week camping with the kids, were leading the afternoon and evening activities.

Ryan and Cory peered at the approaching trio. The two younger girls were pretty and unique in their own right, but in Ryan's opinion, they were merely bookending the masterpiece of Maribeth in the center. Her long braid bounced against her back as she rode, the red ribbon woven through it a stark contrast to the dark locks.

Cory whistled low. "That right there should be a postcard or something."

Ryan nodded his agreement with Cory's appreciation of the exquisite scene. "Or something," he said.

They finally got to the barn, and with Red being no more than fourteen hands high, Nadia easily dismounted and took the horse to his stall. Maribeth also had no trouble with Fallon. But Sam was the tallest of the lot, and Jasmine didn't seem in any hurry to dismount.

Cory moved quickly to her side. "Hey, Jaz, let me help you." He held out a hand and she took it, blushing as she started to slide down. He caught her waist and placed her solidly on the ground.

"Thanks, Cory," she said, then smiled and led the horse toward her stall.

Cory stood there for a moment, then cleared his throat and turned. Ryan, Maribeth and Nadia stood watching, and he knuckled his hat, then went to retrieve his gloves from the hay bale before continuing to unload the feed.

From the look on Maribeth's face, she'd detected the same thing Ryan did from watching the two: there were some feelings there, and they didn't look all that one-sided. But Ryan wasn't the matchmaking type, and he figured with the forwardness he'd experienced from Jasmine earlier today, if Cory waited too long to make his move, she'd probably make hers. So he turned to the first lady he needed to speak to.

"Nadia, I wanted to let you know the money was sent today. You can verify it with the church in Thailand, but the funds for the Women's Lighthouse ministry should be in their account by this evening or at the latest tomorrow morning."

Ryan had expected her to be happy, but he hadn't expected the bear hug he received from the tiny girl.

"Thank you so much, Mr. Brooks. I can't tell you how much good your company's donation will do."

"I appreciate the opportunity to help," he said, accepting the hug and then smiling. "Really, I do." He caught Maribeth wiping her cheeks.

She waited until Nadia turned toward Jasmine and started talking about going to the craft store and then she mouthed, *Not all that bad.*

Ryan held his grin in check while the two girls said their goodbyes to Maribeth, Ryan and Cory so they could "hit the square" for some craft shopping. Cory hauled the last bag into the feed room and then returned Jasmine's wave as the girls left in Nadia's car. Then he looked to Ryan and Maribeth and said, "I'm done here, too, so I'm gonna head on over to the Sanders farm. Y'all have a good day."

"You, too, Cory," Maribeth said.

"And Mr. Brooks, thanks for the advice. I sure do appreciate it."

"You're welcome," Ryan said. "And if you keep working the way you are and follow that plan for getting your degree, I can guarantee an employer will be proud to have you."

Cory smiled broadly. "That's what I'm counting on." Then he climbed in his truck and left.

"You gave Cory advice?" Maribeth asked.

Ryan nodded. "I guess that's what he's calling it. Basically, he told me what he plans to do with his life and asked if I thought it would work, and I told him he's on the right track."

"Coming from an ordinary person, that wouldn't be a big deal," she said, "but coming from the guy who runs Brooks International, I imagine that simple affirmation took on a whole new meaning." Fingers of the afternoon sun filtered through the barn roof and caused her to squint as she looked up at Ryan. "That was really nice of you, by the way."

"From what I hear, I'm not all that bad."

She laughed, a rich, full-bodied laugh that made his smile grow. He truly liked being around her, more than he'd liked being around anyone in a very long time.

"I guess the camp is done for the day?" he asked.

She shook her head. "Not really. But my part of the day is done. Since the kids are tent camping this week, they have activities that go well into the night. Right now, John and Dana are leading them on the supplies and vittles run."

The horses moved around in their stalls, alternating from the water trough to the feed trough, where Cory had left each of them a scoop of sweet feed for an afternoon snack. The sounds of them eating, slurping and neighing mingled in the barn, and Ryan wasn't certain he'd understood Maribeth correctly. "Did you say something about a vittles run?"

She smiled, and he liked the way her cheeks lifted and her eyes danced with the action. "It's one of the trails that we take campers on each week. The trail leads from the ranch to the town square. When campers are spending the night, they can purchase additional camping supplies and snacks for the week in town. They usually pick up some souvenirs, clothes…things like that. Often I sell outfits to the campers, especially those from other cities since they don't have shops like Consigning Women in their hometowns."

"We could do something to alleviate that," Ryan

said, and she'd already started shaking her head before he finished the sentence.

"I'll admit that I've thought about how nice it would be to have the opportunity to make a difference on a bigger scale," she said, and when he opened his mouth to tell her he agreed, she waved a finger to stop him, "but I'm not talking about that with you right now."

He held up his palms. "Hey, you opened the door. I just stepped in."

Another laugh. "Okay. I'll give you that, but we were talking about the supplies and vittles run, not me adding more stores."

"But you did say you'd been thinking about it," he reminded.

"And that's all I'm going to say about it right now. Anyway, since the campers are doing the supplies and vittles run this afternoon, I got finished earlier than usual."

"So, were you planning to go to your store now?" he asked.

She nodded. "I was, but I actually have someone filling in for me for a couple more hours. Why do you ask?"

Whether she realized it or not, she'd opened another door. And like before, Ryan stepped in.

"You've mentioned Jasper Falls, and John and Dana have talked about how amazing it is, but the day I planned to ride out and see it, Onyx decided to give me a detour to the ground." He pointed toward the horses. "What do you think about showing me the falls today?"

Her eyes widened. "You mean on horseback? Because I understand that the doctor has okayed you to walk without the crutches, but you're still healing. And you're wearing a brace."

"I've been cleared for walking and driving," he said. "In my opinion, that probably clears me for horse riding, too."

"I'm not so sure that's anywhere near the same category," she said. "And falling off a horse is what did that to you in the first place." She shook her head. "No, I don't think that's a good idea at all."

Ryan was already moving toward Sam's stall. "It's a great idea," he said, running his hand down the horse's nose. "And you know what they say—if you fall off a horse, you have to get right back on again."

"This is a bad idea," she said, but Ryan was glad to see she had started toward Fallon's stall.

He'd already contemplated how he'd mount Sam. He put his right leg—his only good leg for the time being—in the stirrup and then gently guided his other leg over the horse. It really wasn't that difficult, and it only hurt for the moment that his muscles were lifting the leg over. Piece of cake. In fact, he was already out of the barn and waiting by the time Maribeth and Fallon made an appearance. "You ready?" he asked.

She looked at his leg and frowned. "As long as I know you agree that this is a bad idea."

"No such thing. That's what my father always said, anyway," Ryan said.

"No such thing as what?" she asked, sitting astride Fallon and looking amazing in the glow of the afternoon sunlight. She was so fascinating, and she didn't seem to have a clue, which merely magnified her appeal.

"No such thing as a bad idea," Ryan said, grinning. "So, you gonna lead?"

"I don't know. Maybe I should follow so I'll see when you fall off," she said with a smirk.

He liked her sass, too. "Maybe you should." Then he clicked his tongue against the roof of his mouth, said "Let's go, Sam!" and took off toward the trails with Maribeth following on Fallon. Onyx snarled at them as they passed his section of the field, the stallion irritated by the invasion of his space. Ryan chuckled at the massive animal, then slowed Sam to a trot and then to a walk as they entered the woods. He heard Maribeth talking to Fallon and slowing her down, as well.

"You're crazy, you know that, right?" she asked, bringing Fallon up closer to Sam so they could pass together through the trail.

"Some say that. I prefer outrageous."

She laughed. "You're that, too."

Ryan led Sam through the trail and enjoyed being away from the cabin, inhaling the heady scent of pine mingled with damp earth and blooming wildflowers. They came around the biggest curve in the path to encounter a cascade of rhododendrons and the spot where Ryan had given Dana away on her wedding day. He pulled on the reins. "Whoa, Sam." The horse stopped completely, eager to obey the command and probably as eager to take a little breather.

Maribeth stopped Fallon, as well, and inhaled the incredible fragrance provided by the abundance of vibrant purple, hot-pink and red blooms. "I love this spot."

"I'd planned to ride here again, too, on that day when I ended up blowing out my knee. It doesn't seem that long ago when I walked Dana down this path to marry John. That was a great day, wasn't it?"

She nodded. "The prettiest wedding I've ever been to. I loved the way the whole town lined the path she took to see John. And then these flowers surrounding them while they said their vows… It was perfect."

"I didn't realize you helped her pick out the colors for the wedding until she mentioned it the other day. You did a great job. Of course, you can tell that you have great taste in pairing colors and clothing by your display of talent in your store. That's another reason I was interested in—"

"Don't ruin the moment by talking business," she said, and Ryan grinned.

"Okay, but you know where I was headed."

"Same place it seems all of our conversations head." She gave him a disapproving look as Fallon stuck her nose in a large red bloom and then sneezed loudly. Maribeth stroked the horse's neck. "Easy, girl. Sometimes things that look that good will only get you in trouble."

"Spoken from experience?" he asked.

She shrugged. "It's just the truth."

Ryan suspected there was more truth there than she was willing to talk about, but he was curious. What—or who—had looked too good to Maribeth and gotten her into trouble?

"I, um, have a confession," she said.

Ryan had started to move Sam forward, but gently pulled the reins again to keep her still. "A confession?" he asked, thinking he might actually learn what had looked too good to Maribeth.

"Yes. That day, when I told you I remembered seeing you at the wedding and that you were wearing a navy suit…" She paused, blinked and looked upward as though wondering whether she could tell the rest.

"Yes?" Ryan prompted.

"I remembered your suit. In fact, I remembered it precisely. A gray Brioni Vanquish, and it fit you—" she blushed, and Ryan's pulse stirred "—perfectly." She looked at him. "Okay, that's it. Now I feel better. Let's go on to Jasper Falls." She tapped Fallon's side and the horse turned away from Ryan to allow Maribeth to take the lead.

Ryan watched her, the petite beauty in the saddle leading the way to what he'd heard was one of the most exquisite waterfalls in the South...and pulling his heart in her wake.

This sure felt real. But then again, it'd felt real before, with Nannette. How would he know the difference?

They rounded the next bend in the trail and viewed the scene that Dana had described, a wedding veil of water soaring from the ridge above to tumble into a babbling creek that flowed along the mountain.

"It's beautiful now," Maribeth said, "but it's even prettier when all of those dogwood trees are blooming." She pointed toward the trees.

Ryan couldn't imagine it any more spectacular than it was now; however, that could be because he was seeing it for the first time with Maribeth Walton by his side. Her appeal only magnified each time he was around her, and it reminded him so much of the way he'd initially felt about Nannette that he had to remind himself that this was a different woman, and things might be different with someone else.

Maybe.

If he could put a lock on his skepticism, he would, but his thoughts kept whispering, *fool me once, shame on you, fool me twice, shame on me.* How did a guy know that he wasn't being played?

"It just reminds me of how powerful God is," Maribeth continued.

Ryan tamped down on the old emotions. Maribeth wasn't Nannette, not even remotely like her, because if Ryan had been trying to invest in and build up a business that Nannette Kelly owned, she'd have been all over it and tried to talk him into going even bigger. And she'd do it so that Ryan believed it was his idea. She'd been a master of deceit.

"Don't you think?" Maribeth asked. "All of this—" she held her arms out, tilted her head back and inhaled "—it's like, how could anyone *not* believe in God?"

Ryan let himself relax in the saddle, tilted his own head back to follow her example and inhaled. The earthy scent of the woods combined with the mist of the falls and the faint sounds of birds in the distance did provide a calm reminder that there was a bigger power at work here. And Ryan did believe in God. He simply hadn't seen that God had taken a big interest in his life. His mother had died when Dana was born. His father had been so business focused that his kids were practically raised by strangers. And Ryan had become a virtual carbon copy of his dad. Where was God during all of that?

Yet with his head tilted and his body relaxed, Ryan was fairly certain he sensed Him, right here, right now.

"You feel Him, too, don't you?" she asked.

He nodded, his throat too tight to speak at the moment.

"I know. It's awesome to get outside and really let yourself see everything He's done. It's easy to get so wrapped up in the everyday things in life that we forget to step back and breathe, let ourselves rest and get a chance to truly experience God. That's what working with the camp is doing for me. Every day out here with the kids and with nothing but nature and God surrounding us, it's so easy to remember that He did this."

Ryan swallowed, found his voice. "I see why you volunteer now."

"That phrase that you said earlier, it comes from one of the verses we teach the campers each week."

"What phrase?" Ryan asked.

"The one that says if you fall off a horse, you should get right back on," she said. "It comes from Proverbs, chapter twenty-four, verse sixteen, 'For though the righteous fall seven times, they rise again, but the wicked stumble when calamity strikes.'"

"Does that mean I'm going to fall off a horse six more times?" Ryan asked.

"I don't know, but if you're thinking about falling off today, wait until we get closer to the barn. I don't think I can carry you all the way back." Then she laughed so hard that Fallon took a step backward. "Sorry, girl," she said, patting the palomino's throat.

"You're very funny," Ryan said, but he couldn't stop grinning. This, in fact, was the most fun he'd had since he arrived in Claremont.

"I'm sorry. Sometimes I tease too much. I don't mean anything by it—promise."

He looked at her, the dark eyes that were warm and friendly, the smile that tugged at her lips and the playful way she bantered with him. This was what a real relationship would feel like, he supposed. Similar to the interaction he'd witnessed between Chad and Jessica

Martin when they'd brought Nathan and Lainey to the ranch. He'd thought he would like to have a relationship like that, and now that he was getting a glimpse into how it would feel, he did like it, very much.

"What?" she asked, and Ryan realized he'd been staring.

"Should we let them get a drink while we're here?" he asked, ready to change the subject.

"Sure." She glanced at the water. "We can dismount if you want and let them get their fill of the water while we relax a little while." She looked at his leg. "Or maybe that isn't a good idea."

"Actually, I think it might feel good to get off and straighten it out for a few minutes before we ride back."

"You sure?" she asked.

To show he was, he pressed his right leg in the stirrup and maneuvered his left leg over, holding the saddle tightly to keep from putting all of his weight on his left leg when it hit the ground. It was painful, but he managed, and for a little more time with Maribeth, enjoying this exquisite scene, it was worth it.

Apparently, it took him longer to get down than he realized, because by the time he got his balance, she was at his side, her hand steadying his arm. "You okay?" she asked.

"Yeah, I'm okay," he said as the horses moved to the water and began to drink their fill. In fact, he was more than okay. He felt more alive than he had in years.

Maribeth glanced at her hand on his arm. It'd been so natural to reach for him. The sleeve of his shirt separated her palm from his forearm, but his warmth permeated the boundary, and she didn't find it overly easy to slide her hand away. "I'm glad you're okay," she said, and walked toward a large flat rock near the stream. "Want to sit over here?" she asked.

"Sure." He walked slowly, his leg appearing to move stiffly.

Maribeth found herself holding her breath as he worked his way across the soft earth to finally reach the smooth rock where she sat. She didn't want him to fall, and she knew that riding the horses out here and having Ryan navigate the uneven terrain to sit near the stream wasn't the best way to keep that from happening. But she did want him to sit beside her, wanted him to enjoy the serenity that she experienced every day beside the waterfall. She wanted him to feel God, the way she did every time she came to Jasper Falls. "Still okay?" she asked, as he sat beside her on the large, smooth rock.

"Never better," he said, wincing a little as he straightened his left leg in front of him.

"Okay, I can tell you're lying, but I won't call you on it," she said.

"I think you just did, but I'll ignore it," he said, grinning.

"Works for me," she said, shoving him playfully with her shoulder and enjoying the smile she received in return. She pointed to the grouping of tents on the other side of the water. "Over there is where the kids and the chaperones will camp tonight. John did a great job clearing out an area for the campsites without distorting the natural surroundings. I remember when they were talking about putting campsites here. I asked Dana if they were trying to preserve the natural state of the woods, the falls and everything, and she said that was a top priority."

His mouth flattened. "I wish I'd have paid more attention back then, when Dana was so excited about the camping facilities they were creating for church groups."

"You didn't want the camp here?" she asked, surprised.

He smiled. "Isn't that just like my sister, not to tell you about that? No, I wasn't on board at all. In fact, you could say I was her main opposition, a thorn in her side as she tried to get Brooks International to back the investment for the dude ranch. The marketing analysis didn't lend credence to the success of a dude ranch in Alabama."

"But I'm assuming you agreed to it eventually, or it wouldn't be here, right?" she asked.

He took a deep breath, readjusted his leg and consequently slid a little closer to Maribeth. She didn't mind at all. "Yeah, she won me over before it was all said and done, and I'm glad now. This was undoubtedly a sound investment."

"God was behind it," Maribeth said. "He had to be. He knew that this place could touch a lot of lives, and when He's behind something, then it works."

"You really believe that, don't you?"

"With all of my heart. I turned away from Him once in my life, and if I'd have just listened to Him, or my family, I wouldn't have gone through—" She realized he'd gone completely silent, listening to her every word, and also that she was telling him more than she intended. "Anyway, everything is better when you have God where He belongs—in control."

"I wouldn't mind it if you decided to tell me the rest," he said softly. "Whatever you were about to say."

She swallowed, uncertain how to respond. She'd finally distanced herself from that awful time in her life, and she didn't want to talk about it, wasn't even sure why she'd brought it up. Except she wanted to talk to Ryan, to be open with him, for some reason.

"It's okay," he said. "You don't have to if you aren't ready to share."

"Thanks," she said. Yes, she might decide to confide in him eventually, but those old fears were still unsettling enough to keep her silent for the time being.

Ryan looked disappointed, but he didn't try to coax her anymore. Instead, he closed his eyes and leaned his head back to enjoy the mist from the falls brushing against his skin, and Maribeth found herself mesmerized by the image, like a sculpture of a beautiful male, enjoying the coolness of the falls on a heated afternoon.

"This is incredible," he said.

"I know." She shifted, uncomfortable at her unabashed gawking, and when Ryan opened his eyes, she glanced toward the creek.

"What is it?" he asked.

She'd been thinking about this ever since their interaction in the barn. "I wanted to ask you about something, but the only reason I even know about it is because of my eavesdropping earlier, so since I shouldn't have heard, then maybe I shouldn't ask…."

"Okay, you've got my attention," he said, "and there's no way you can go without asking whatever it is now. That'd just be cruel."

She turned toward him again and said, "Jasmine said something about a girl that the magazines said you were going to marry, or that you secretly married."

His jaw tensed, and he undoubtedly knew where this conversation was headed and wasn't eager to go there.

But Maribeth wanted to know, so she forged ahead. "Did you marry someone, and it went badly? Is that why you said that Jasmine deserved someone who would give his heart to her, and that was more than you could give?"

He turned to face her and then winced.

"I'm sorry, I shouldn't have asked," she said, feeling guilty for causing him pain. "I'm being nosy, and usually that's not my nature at all. In fact, I hate it when someone asks me about things I don't want to talk about. Why should I think that you're any different?"

"Hey, I was just moving my leg," he said. "If I turn it the wrong way, my knee hurts. That doesn't have anything to do with your question. You want to know, so I want to tell you."

Maribeth could sense the seriousness of what he was about to say. He'd decided to confide in her, to trust her, and she was incredibly touched that he didn't simply tell her he wasn't ready to talk, the way she'd told him a few minutes ago.

"I met Nannette three years ago. I was twenty-seven and she was twenty-five. She was from South Carolina but going to school in Chicago, attending the School of the Art Institute. I saw her for the first time at one of the art galas."

"I believe I have a photo on my wall of you at one of those," she said.

He nodded. "I don't miss their events. My father was a big supporter of the Art Institute, and on that eve- ning, we were attending a gala there that showcased the school's senior artists. I was admiring one of her paintings when she walked up and introduced herself as the struggling artist who created that masterpiece."

"Did she know who you were?" Maribeth asked.

"You see, that's a good question, because at the time she acted as though she didn't, and I really liked that. I introduced myself as Ryan and didn't provide a last name. We chatted, and I'll be honest, I was taken with her that first night. I'm pretty sure she knew."

"Most people know you from the tabloids," Maribeth said.

"Yeah, I get that now. But back then, before my father passed away, I wasn't as notably in the public eye. I rarely made the tabloids, unless it was a photo of me with my father, so there was the off chance that she didn't recognize me," he said.

"Which was what you wanted," Maribeth said.

"Like I said, I didn't provide a last name. And it was kind of nice, thinking that she was interested in me regardless of the fact that my last name was Brooks."

Shock rippled through Maribeth. Did he not realize how exceptional his looks were, or how easy he was to talk to, or how a woman could get lost in the sound of his voice and his laugh? "You think she wouldn't have been interested enough to talk to you if she hadn't known your last name?"

"That's the thing," he said. "I'll never know. That night she joked about the whole starving-artist persona and said she didn't mind being poor forever if she were able to convey her feelings on a canvas." He laughed. "I fell for it."

"Are you sure she wasn't telling you the truth?"

"Oh, yeah, I'm sure," he said, the pain of those words evident in his tone. "We dated nearly two years.

Naturally, I told her who I was after the first few dates, and she acted as though it didn't matter whether I had money or not, whether I would inherit my father's business or not. She pretended she loved me, that I was the only man she could ever love, and that she would stay by my side forever."

"And then?" Maribeth whispered, suspecting she knew what happened. "Jasmine said something about you secretly marrying? Did you marry her?"

He shook his head. "No. That was merely tabloid gossip, fodder to sell more copies. It wasn't true. We never married. But it's almost laughable how close they were to the truth. They said we secretly married and then had it annulled because she met Alex Sharp at a party I hosted. At the time he played third base for the Cubs. Since then, he's been traded to the Yankees. Anyway, they said we annulled our marriage when she met him at a Brooks party."

"And that was close to the truth?" Maribeth asked. She scooted nearer to him on the rock and placed her hand over his, her small fingers sliding easily between his longer ones. "How was it close to the truth?"

"On the night of that party, a celebration party for a resort we'd purchased in Oahu, she met Alex. Like me, he became infatuated with her from the moment he saw her, but unlike me, he made his move swiftly. From the photos the tabloids caught, after the party ended and I took her to her apartment, she went back out…with Alex. Seems he took her on some sort of *Pretty Woman* type of shopping spree that night, had the stores open for her and basically gave her everything she wanted. Then he told her he wanted to give her everything she wanted for life, and she said yes. Or that's the line they gave the press when asked about their rapid engagement and the wedding in Jamaica that occurred merely two months after the night of that party."

And Maribeth had thought *her* experience with the tabloids was bad. His was so much worse. If she hadn't started avoiding even glancing at the papers at the supermarket after her own ordeal, she, like Jasmine, might also have known about Nannette's deception. And Ryan's pain. "Oh, Ryan, I'm so sorry."

"Wait," he said. "It gets better. The reason that I said the tabloids nearly got it right, though, was because I'd planned to propose that night. I had the ring in my pocket and was ready to get down on one knee, the whole nine yards. But the timing never seemed right. And then she went out with Sharp, and I knew she'd never been in love with me. She was in love with the money." His smile was forced. "There are a whole lot of people out there who can fall in love with the money."

She slid her hand to his wrist and twisted her body to face him. "It's terrible when you think someone loves you, and when you love them, and then—" she blinked and her tears fell free "—you find out that they don't."

Ryan looked directly at her now, and she knew he undoubtedly saw the pain in her eyes, but she didn't look away this time. He'd opened up to her, and she could feel herself wanting to do the same. But what would happen if she did? What if the two of them did become close and then the truth of her past hit the tabloids once more? Because that's what would happen if she let herself become involved with someone like Ryan. She couldn't go through that again.

She couldn't.

"You've felt that before, too, haven't you?" he asked. "You thought someone loved you, really believed that they cared about you, and then you found out that they didn't."

She couldn't deny it, so she nodded. "And the worst part is, once you've been treated so badly, it's difficult to open your heart again, isn't it?"

She hadn't intended to, but she'd moved a little closer as she spoke.

"It is difficult," he whispered, "nearly impossible." And before she could stop him from doing what seemed as natural as the waterfall, the woods and the creek surrounding them, he eased even closer and pressed his lips to hers.

Chapter Nine

Ryan woke bright and early the next day, but he called and moved his therapy session to noon. He hadn't stopped thinking about the time he'd spent with Maribeth, and he didn't want to wait until the end of the day to see her again.

Before their conversation—and that kiss—he'd known he was attracted to the lady, but he hadn't been certain whether it was only a physical attraction or perhaps an intellectual attraction, because of the gem of an idea she had for her business. But the more he was with her and got to know her, the more he realized he was smitten with the entire package that was Maribeth Walton. Emotionally. Physically. Even spiritually. Because her intense faith had him contemplating his own relationship with God.

Ryan sat near the window drinking his coffee and watching for Maribeth to arrive. John and Dana had camped with the group at Jasper Falls last night, so Ryan had the place to himself, which was fine. It gave him time to collect his thoughts and to consider the feelings an intriguing brunette had stirred up yesterday afternoon.

He'd already started considering ways that they could move forward with a relationship, if indeed that was where this was headed. At first he thought it wouldn't work. She lived in Claremont, had her business here and undeniably loved the small-town life. His business—his life—was in Chicago.

Ryan reached the bottom of the cup of coffee. He stood and made his way to the kitchen, his steps a bit off-rhythm against the hardwood floor due to his brace. But it was better than yesterday. Each day, thanks to his therapy, had been better than the one before. Soon he'd be done with rehab completely and able to go home. Back to living.

He poured another cup of coffee and thought about how relaxing mornings were on the farm. Taking time to drink coffee, scan the fields, think about the day to come. In Chicago, his alarm went off and he went through the rushed morning routine that involved a 5:30 a.m. workout with his personal trainer, a scalding-hot shower, a protein bar with his coffee, dressing in a power suit and then heading to the office for another round of meetings, agreements and compromises.

Ryan inhaled the coffee, took another drink and decided to do something he hadn't done in…probably forever.

Dear God, if You hear me, and if You are in on all of this, whatever is happening to me now, being in Claremont and meeting Maribeth and starting to think about a relationship again, starting to think about You, then I want to say thank You. Amen.

It wasn't much of a prayer, he supposed, but it was

better than nothing. He'd have to get used to praying. It was probably like anything else a person did and would only get better with determination and practice. His father had drilled that into him repeatedly over the years, and that was one philosophy of Lawrence Brooks's that Ryan would never disagree with.

Not that he disagreed with much of his father's philosophy.

But if Ryan did give faith a try, and he'd already decided he wanted to at least give it consideration, then that was completely opposite to what Lawrence Brooks had taught him growing up. Ryan's father was a fierce proponent of "self-made, self-earned." He'd never thanked God for anything.

"Daddy changed in the end. He realized he had a lot of things backwards."

Dana's words echoed through Ryan's thoughts. He'd scoffed at her insistence that their father had had that change of heart toward the end of his life. But in the brief time that Ryan had been in Claremont, and particularly the time he'd been around Maribeth, he'd felt his own heart changing.

Maybe his father had found a belief—and a need—for a higher power in the end.

The sound of a car engine caught Ryan's attention, and he left the kitchen and made his way to the front window in time to see Maribeth climbing from her car. Something caught the morning sunlight and sparkled as she moved. Ryan squinted to see the source of the glimmer and found himself admiring the unique creation by the woman who could, if she wanted, dress the stars on a budget. A floral-print shirt, cream with peach flowers, matching cream-colored cowboy hat with a peach sash, worn jeans tucked into equally worn boots…and a scarf threaded through the belt loops with those sparkling stones that captured the sunshine dangling from the ends.

Ryan set his coffee mug on the table as she disappeared into the barn and then he headed out the door. He skipped the ramp and took the steps instead, the unlocked brace cinching with each step. He was glad when he reached the ground. Yesterday, riding Sam had been effortless once he was in the saddle. Mounting and dismounting were the hard parts, but riding had been a piece of cake and even more enjoyable with Maribeth riding Fallon at his side.

The soft earth gave with every step toward the barn, and Ryan was reminded of that night in the rain when his crutch broke in two and Maribeth rushed to his side. Smiling at the memory of himself covered with mud on the ground, he continued his progress. Eventually, she exited the barn and moved to the fence with something in her hand. She climbed onto the bottom rail so she could lean over as she held out the treat, a carrot, and attempted to coax Onyx over.

Ryan continued his trek and finally picked up the pace when the ground became more compact beside the barn. As he neared, he heard her words to the stallion.

"Come on, big guy. You know you want this. Those kids today are gonna want to see you up close and personal. And I've gotta figure out a way to make that happen. You want a snack, don't ya?"

Ryan had never noticed how strongly Maribeth's Southern accent came into play when she spoke, but there were hardly any words in her vocabulary that came out as one syllable, each sentence sounding like a melody.

"Do y'all want his carrot?" she called to Sam and Fallon, who were nearing the fence and ready to take Onyx's discards.

Y'all. Ryan took in the exquisite lady who could easily adorn a Maldives postcard and could also use the word *y'all* (with two syllables, no less) in a sentence.

She pressed the carrot against the top fence rail to break it in two and then held her palms out to her new best friends. Sam and Fallon wasted no time getting their treats. She rubbed each of their noses and then showed them her palms were empty. "Sorry, nothing else right now, but I'll give you another one when the kids get to the barn after their breakfast." Then, after Sam and Fallon realized there was no more food and moved back to the pasture, she leaned over the fence again. "You missed out. You do know that, don't you?"

Onyx tilted his head, then turned away to look the opposite direction, putting his backside toward Maribeth.

"Well, that wasn't very nice," she said.

Ryan laughed and she jumped, nearly losing her balance on the fence rail.

Her dark eyes widened. "Hey, how long have you been there?"

"Long enough to see how cute you are trying to bribe a stallion."

A slight flush tinted her cheeks and the area just beneath her throat, and Ryan wondered if it was because he startled her, or because she was remembering the kiss they shared yesterday afternoon. Or both. Then she lifted an arched brow and pointed a warning finger toward him. "You should tell people when you're sneaking up on them."

"I think that'd defy the whole definition of sneaking, don't you?" he asked.

Her mouth twitched, and he could tell she was fighting a smile, but she reined it in. "Well, you should have let me know you were walking over."

"It took me long enough that I thought you would've noticed, but you were too into trying to win Onyx's favor to pay attention to the guy semi-limping from the house."

"You're moving better every day." She stepped down from the fence rail and looked at the big black horse, a good seventeen hands tall, only a few feet away from the fence and still facing the opposite direction. "You'd think he was showing me his backside on purpose," she said.

Ryan laughed. "Maybe you didn't offer him the kind of treat he wanted. He's partial to green apples. So is Fallon, if you want to get down to it, but she'll eat anything. Onyx is more particular." He nodded toward the barn. "Dana has taught me a few things about their favorite treats. She keeps a burlap sack of the apples inside the tack room. Want me to get you one?"

"No, I know where they are. I've been giving them to Fallon, and I actually tried to get Onyx to eat one a couple of days ago," she said, easily climbing through the fence rails and then starting toward the barn. "But he gave me the same treatment I'm getting right now." She smirked and pointed to the horse's tail.

Ryan laughed. "Want me to try?"

"I'm surprised you're so willing to give him what

he wants since he's the one who put you in that cast," she called from inside the barn.

"He didn't do it," Ryan said, watching her return with a couple of Granny Smith apples. "Whatever spooked him put me in the cast. I don't have any problem with Onyx. He's got attitude, but I never met a stallion that didn't. And I'll ride him again one day. You can count on that."

"Sounds like Onyx isn't the only thing here right now with attitude," she said.

Ryan knuckled his cowboy hat like a guy who wore one on a regular basis, and it didn't feel all that awkward. Then he winked at her and was rewarded with her flushed cheeks.

"You're too much," she said, shaking her head.

"I try." He pointed to the black stallion making his way toward the fence. "Look, attitude or not, he wants one of those apples."

Maribeth held out her hand toward the impressive animal. Ryan heard her breath hitch when Onyx eased toward her and brought his velvety lips against her palm. "Oh, my," she whispered. "The kids will love having something as beautiful as you come up close. You really aren't anything to be afraid of, are you?"

"No, he isn't," Ryan said, "and I agree with your earlier statement, too."

"What's that?" she asked.

"He isn't the only thing around here with attitude." He tilted his head toward Maribeth, and she laughed.

"You're saying *I* have a problem with my attitude?" she questioned.

"I didn't say that. I said you have attitude. There's a difference," he clarified.

She gave Onyx the second apple and he hurriedly chomped it away. "You make me laugh," she said.

"You talking to the horse now, or me?"

As if proving the statement, her laughter rang out. "Both!" When Onyx finished the apple and turned to make his way toward the water trough, Maribeth climbed over the fence to stand beside Ryan. "I didn't think you'd be here this morning. I thought you'd be at your rehab therapy."

"I moved it to the middle of the day," he said. She was standing near, so near that he could feel the warmth of her body against his side. And his eyes wandered to her mouth.

She ran her teeth over her lower lip and glanced toward the woods. "John and Dana will be bringing the kids here soon. They're spending the morning fishing over at the pond and are coming by the barn on the way. That's where I'm meeting them."

"When will they be here?" he asked, their faces mere inches apart now.

"Any minute," she whispered, and Ryan liked the fact that she also focused on his lips, and then her eyes slid closed.

He kissed her slowly, taking his time to enjoy the caress of her mouth against his, and he didn't attempt to stop until he heard the sound of horses' hooves in the distance.

When he ended the kiss, Maribeth groaned her disapproval and he laughed, then brushed one more soft kiss across her mouth before saying, "They're almost here."

Apparently reality set in, because her eyes popped open and she whirled to see the group, so busy laughing and chatting as they neared that they didn't pay any attention to the couple kissing by the barn. However, the all-knowing look on Dana's face—and John's, for that matter—said his sister and brother-in-law hadn't missed a thing.

"Ryan, I thought you'd be at therapy now," Dana said.

"Moved it to the afternoon," he said, not making any effort to put any distance between himself and Maribeth.

"O-kay," she said, grinning.

Ryan had no doubt his sister had hoped something would happen between him and her friend. So she should be happy now, because something was definitely happening.

"We were stopping here to pick up Maribeth, Nadia and Jasmine, right?" John asked.

"Nadia texted me that they were running a little late," Maribeth said.

"You want to stay here and wait on them? When they get here y'all can meet us down at the pond," he continued. "That'll give me a chance to distribute the rods and bait."

"Sure," Maribeth said.

John led the way with the kids and chaperones following, and Dana waited to bring up the rear. She brought her horse near the fence, glanced to make sure the campers were out of earshot and then said, "I'm glad you two are…talking."

Ryan knew she'd probably seen them more than talking, but he simply said, "We are, too."

"You never cease to surprise me, Ryan," she added.

Ryan grinned. "Thanks."

Then the last camper crested the hill that led to the pond, and Dana trotted after him.

"You've surprised me a bit, too," Maribeth said softly.

"Should I take that as a compliment?" he asked, touching his finger to her lower lip. He wanted to kiss her again, but he heard the sound of a car coming up the driveway, so he tenderly traced her lip with his finger, then pulled it away.

"It's a compliment," she said.

"Then thanks."

She laughed, and as the car appeared, she took a step away. "I guess I better get ready to start the camp day."

"One thing first," he said.

"What's that?"

"I wanted you to know that I get this." He pointed toward her outfit.

"You get what?" she asked, undeniably confused.

"Your clothes. I realized that when you work in your store, you wear outfits designed to match those of celebrities, but until today, I didn't realize that you do that with your casual clothes, too. It's ingenious."

"Ingenious?" she asked, a soft chuckle trilling through the word. "And how can you be so sure that this is a celebrity's ensemble?" She waved her hand down the length of her body, and the more he studied the clothes, the more he knew for certain that he'd seen something very similar before.

"Because I know whose outfit you're wearing."

Nadia had parked her car, and she and Jasmine got out and started walking toward them. Obviously they'd heard the comment.

"You know whose outfit that is?" Nadia asked. She

examined Maribeth's peach shirt, worn jeans, boots and cowboy hat while Maribeth shook her head as if saying there was no way Ryan would get this right.

"I don't know this one," Jasmine said, confirming Ryan's belief that Maribeth did, in fact, mimic the celebrities in her casual wear, too.

"I've got an idea," Ryan said, tapping his chin as though he really was putting thought into what he was about to say, when in truth he already had his mind made up.

Maribeth wasn't fooled. "I'm thinking you're up to something, but I'll bite. What's your idea?"

Jasmine and Nadia grinned and stopped walking toward the barn. Apparently they wanted to hear what Ryan had to say, too.

"If I tell you whose outfit you have on today, will you agree to have coffee with me after church tonight?" He realized he'd just asked her out in front of the two girls and that it probably would have been smarter to ask her privately. So he added, "We could talk about my ideas for growing your business."

Jasmine stood directly behind Maribeth, so that Maribeth couldn't see her give a thumbs-up sign to Ryan. He was glad the girl was on board with this. After the awkward flirtation yesterday, he was a little surprised. But then again, she'd seemed to bounce back rather quickly when Cory Shields had shown interest.

"I don't think I want to discuss growing my business," she said, and he didn't like the fact that her tone wasn't as happy as it'd been a moment ago. But Ryan did want to grow her business. However, he now also wanted to grow their relationship and see where this might lead.

"Okay, even if we don't talk business, will you at least have coffee with me and talk about something else after church tonight?"

Maribeth's eyes widened. "Does that mean you're going to church tonight?"

"I'd already decided that," he said. "Seems all these people praying for me have me thinking about it, and I decided if I'm thinking about faith, I might as well see where I stand. Where better to figure that out than at church?"

Her smile stretched into her cheeks. "Where better?" she echoed. And then she said, "So you think you can tell me whose outfit I'm wearing, and if you get it right, then I'll go have coffee with you after church… and we might—or might not—talk about business."

"That's the deal," he said.

"And what if you're wrong?" she asked.

"Then I promise I won't ever ask you about growing your business again," he said, knowing he would not be wrong.

"Okay then, deal. Whose outfit am I wearing?" Maribeth asked. Her smile looked triumphant now, as though she knew he'd never get this right.

Never underestimate a Brooks. A Lawrence Brooks saying that Maribeth should've paid attention to.

He cut the preamble and went straight to the chase. "Sandra Bullock in *Hope Floats,* right down to the worn cowboy boots. And, in case you're curious, I can also tell you what she wore to the accompanying premiere."

"You're amazing," Jasmine said, and Ryan thought he might have messed up by trying to impress Maribeth in front of this particular female.

"Wait and let's see if he gets this right," Maribeth said. "Because that would be amazing. And I know what she wore, because I have the photo from her at that premiere on the wall in the store. So you tell me, what did she wear?"

"It was a black pantsuit, with some kind of strapless lace top underneath. I have no idea what designer, but I know that's what she wore." He waited a second while Nadia and Jasmine both looked toward Maribeth for the answer.

"Is that right?" Nadia asked.

"Yes," Maribeth said, and to Ryan's delight, she sounded impressed. He'd have to start studying the premiere pictures in the tabloids so he could impress her more often. "How did you know?" she asked.

He leaned against the fence and took the weight off his braced leg. "Dana has always adored Sandra Bullock," he explained. "We were teens when that movie came out, and our father knew she'd want the first chance to see it, so he took us. I was at that premiere."

"Of course you were," Maribeth said with a laugh. "Your sister was right. You are full of surprises."

"So, coffee after church? I saw a little coffee shop on the square the other night when Dana and I were there."

She nodded. "That sounds great."

Jasmine held up two thumbs and then Nadia said, "That was pretty cool, Mr. Brooks, how you guessed the outfit and all. I don't suppose you've ever been asked out on a date quite like that before, have you, Maribeth?"

Ryan waited to see if she'd say that it wasn't a date, but she surprised him when she answered, "No, I haven't, and you're right. It is pretty cool."

Nadia and Jasmine turned and chatted about *Hope Floats,* how they'd both seen it on television and how cute they thought Harry Connick Jr. was in the movie while Ryan stayed beside the woman who, in his astute opinion, would give Sandra Bullock a run for her money as the most spectacular female in a peach floral shirt, jeans and boots.

"Pretty cool, huh?" he repeated.

She laughed. "And modest. Don't forget modest."

"By all means, modest." He liked this, teasing each other, learning each other and planning something that she considered a date. Worked for him. "So, what time does church start?"

"Seven o'clock," she answered.

"Want me to pick you up at six forty-five? Might as well ride together," he said.

"You sure you can drive? I know you said the doctor cleared it, but…" She pointed to his brace-covered leg.

"Shifting gears would be difficult, but Dana's car is an automatic." He pointed to his sister's car, parked beneath the oak tree in front of the house. "So we're good to go."

Her cheeks were still flushed, and the tinge had traveled to the vee of her shirt when he'd guessed her outfit correctly. She was so beautiful when she blushed, the sweetness of the action conveying the honesty and natural beauty of the woman. The breeze from the mountain caused one long dark lock to brush across her face, and she pushed it out of the way to give Ryan one more smile before she said, "We're good to go," and then turned and entered the barn.

Chapter Ten

Maribeth always loved the Wednesday-night Bible study, because it rejuvenated her spirit and prepared her for the remainder of the week. But tonight's would be even more special, because of Ryan.

He knocked on the back door of Consigning Women, which happened to be the door leading to her kitchen, promptly at six forty-five. Maribeth answered and found he'd dressed in a black Western shirt, khakis and boots. She nodded her approval. "You'll blend well."

"I'll be honest, I wasn't sure what to wear to a church service, so I asked Dana for advice. I'm guessing she didn't steer me wrong."

"No, she didn't." If Maribeth were describing his attire for one of her clothing ensembles, she'd say something like, *A classic black Western shirt and khakis are best suited for an athletic build, a muscular physique that isn't too over the top. Perfect for a guy who wants to make a statement but isn't lacking confidence.*

She blinked and shook the blurb away. That wasn't the type of thing she'd say. If this outfit were in her store, she'd be pairing it with what celebrity wore it best. *This vintage Western shirt, khakis and boots are perfectly suited for*—Maribeth drew a blank for what star might be wearing this attire, because the only one she believed it perfectly suited…was standing in her doorway. And waiting for her to say something.

"Oh, I'm sorry," she said. "You ready to go?"

He smiled. "Not until you let me guess."

"Guess?"

He pointed to the simple ultrapale blue dress that she loved. "Cameron Diaz?"

She shook her head. "Katie Holmes, at the premiere of *The Kennedys*."

He nodded. "I should've thought of that. It does have a Jackie Kennedy simple-yet-classic look. I like it. A lot."

"I do, too," she said, then picked up the Bibles she'd placed on the table by the door. "I got an extra Bible in case you need one."

"Dana actually gave me one to use tonight, and then I walked out without it. So, thanks. I'm sure that'll be handy, right?"

"Right." Maribeth had worried about assuming he wouldn't have a Bible of his own, but he didn't seem insulted at all that she had one for him; on the contrary, his appreciation of her gesture touched her heart.

Ryan walked beside her, his hand against the small of her back as he gently guided her to the car. Then he opened her door and waited. "All set?" he asked as she clicked the seat belt into place.

"Yes, thanks."

Then he circled the car and climbed in.

"I've got to admit, I'm a little nervous about this church thing, but I'm ready to give it a try," he said as he backed out of the parking space and began the short drive to Claremont Community Church.

"Have you been to church before? Or is that something I shouldn't ask?" She didn't want to insult him, really she didn't, but it surprised her that someone could be thirty years old and never have attended church.

"Weddings and funerals," he said. "So this'll be something new." He pulled up to the four-way stop at Maple and waited for two other cars to take their turns. "My father never wanted to rely on anything but himself," he said, "and he didn't want us relying on anything else, either."

"That's...sad," she said, when that was the only word that came to mind. She squinted as the setting sun got so bright ahead of them that she could just barely make out Ryan's face.

He leaned toward her, and for a moment she thought he would kiss her here, at the four-way stop, while cars continued to line up. But he eased his hand in front of her face, reached for the visor and pulled it down to block the bright light from her eyes. "Better?" he asked.

She swallowed. "Yes, thanks."

Then he took her hand in his, folded his fingers over hers and said, "Let's think about tonight and not worry about what I have or haven't done in the past."

"That sounds great," she said, but her mind kept wondering what his life had been like as a child growing up without faith. And she kept coming back to that same word. *Sad*.

Ryan hadn't known what he'd expected from his first trip to church, but it wasn't this. Practically the entire town filled the tiny white-steepled building. And everyone made an effort to come by and say hello, not because he was Ryan Brooks of Brooks International, but because he was Ryan, Dana's brother, John's brother-in-law, Abi's uncle. And he loved every handshake, every introduction, every friendly smile. There was nothing fake about the people of Claremont. They weren't looking for an investor, didn't ask for a loan, didn't care what he had sitting in the bank or logged on his books. They simply wanted to get to know *him*.

What a concept.

And the woman by his side only made the night better. Yes, the dress she wore had a Jackie Kennedy style, but the style he'd come to adore was all her own. Tonight her hair was held back by a pale blue satin band in a manner probably worn by the famed first lady, but it suited Maribeth, too. Anything, Ryan concluded, would suit Maribeth.

During the lesson taught by Brother Henry, she guided Ryan when he looked for the Scriptures without drawing attention to the fact that he was somewhat lost when it came to Bible knowledge. He had no idea whether a book was in the Old Testament or the New, but he did understand tonight's subject of prayer. And he knew God had put it on his heart to come tonight because He knew what Ryan needed most: Him.

Each passage resonated within Ryan, not only showing the power and necessity of a person's ability to pray to God, but also the simplicity of the act. God wanted to be talked to. He wanted to be Lord, friend, father. And there was no right or wrong to prayer. You simply talked to Him, He listened and He answered.

A comfort washed over Ryan as he put the pieces together and realized that he'd never once turned to God for help, not as a kid, when he'd resented the fact that he didn't have a mother, not as a teen, when he'd wanted to spend time with his dad and his dad was too busy building a *Fortune* 500 company to go fishing with his son, and not when his father had died and the weight of running that company fell on Ryan's shoulders. He'd been alone for all of it, and he didn't have to be.

If only he'd realized it sooner.

"Ryan, you okay?" Dana's voice surprised him, and he looked up to see her standing in front of his pew. Apparently he'd been so absorbed in the sermon, and then the last song, that he hadn't realized they'd been dismissed. He also hadn't realized how tightly he'd grasped Maribeth's tiny hand. He looked at where their fingers were joined and loosened his grip. "Sorry about that."

She smiled, her dark eyes warm with compassion. "Don't be." Then, as though she knew he wasn't quite ready to face Dana's questions about what had his heart clenching in his chest, she said, "Ready to go get that coffee?"

He continued holding her hand and let her lead the way out of the church while they politely said their goodbyes to everyone and headed toward the car. Outside, when the summer-night air touched his skin, Ryan felt as though he could breathe again, and he took control, ushering her to the passenger side of the car and letting her in.

At the church, Ryan's phone hadn't had service, but about midway between the church and the square that must have changed, because it buzzed wildly with alerts of missed calls and texts. But Ryan was done with business today. Something had happened at the church; his spirit had been moved, he supposed. He'd heard the phrase before and never thought it realistic...until now.

Maribeth didn't say anything until they pulled into the parking lot and he turned off the car. But Ryan knew what she was thinking, and he wasn't the type to skirt the facts.

"Was it that obvious, the fact that I was having a tough time at the church?" he asked simply.

"Just a little," she said, her voice soft and warm and perfect. "Brother Henry has a way of doing that, you know, touching what needs to be touched and evoking emotions that maybe we're trying to keep hidden," she said.

They sat in the parked car in silence for a moment, and then she said, "If you'd rather not do the coffee tonight, we can wait until another time."

"No, I want to," he said. "And I want to tell you what all was going on back there, what had me so worked up."

"Okay then." She reached for her door handle and he attempted to hurry and help her out. But he couldn't move quickly enough with the brace, and she was waiting on him when he got to the other side.

"Falling down on my job already," he said, glad to feel himself relaxing and able to smile again.

"That's okay. I can open my own door."

"But you won't have to," he said.

Then he put an arm around her, and it felt as natural as if he'd been doing it his entire life, and they walked to the front of her store and then across the square toward the Grind.

Maribeth couldn't remember a guy ever treating her with such kindness and tenderness on a date, let alone a first date. She wasn't certain exactly when it had happened, if it was when he admitted he'd never had faith in his world but was willing to look for it now, or when he'd sweetly moved her visor to shield her eyes from the sun, or when he'd squeezed her hand in church as the sermon touched his soul, but at some point during the night she'd realized that her heart had already fallen. She was in love with Ryan Brooks.

"What about here?" he asked, pointing to one of the wrought iron bistro tables on the Grind's patio.

"Perfect." She sat across from him and within minutes they'd placed their order and soon had steaming mugs of coffee, black for him and a white-chocolate mocha for her, in front of them on the table.

He ran a hand down his face and then rubbed his chin, like a guy who was about to deliver bad news, except Maribeth suspected the news wasn't about anything in the present, but in his past. She knew what that was like, and she thought she'd tell him about her history, too. If she were to truly give him her heart, she'd want him to know everything. But tonight was about Ryan. Church had touched him, and he wanted to open up. She'd let him, and soon, when the time was right, she'd open up, too.

"In all my years of attending seminars my father recommended on self-evaluation, running a successful business, creating your professional destiny, nothing has affected me the way Brother Henry's lesson did tonight. I think it was because what he was saying is that it isn't merely up to me. I'm not the one in control, and I shouldn't want to be. And after thinking about it—really examining how I've lived my life, particularly since my father died—I don't want to feel I'm on my own." He shook his head. "I can command a boardroom, keep an audience's attention for an hour-long speech with no problem at all, but I honestly can't convey what I'm feeling right now."

"That's because you're feeling faith. God. The truth that the world doesn't revolve around you," she said. "Wait. That didn't come out right."

He laughed, and she loved the way it filled the air and seemed to release the tension completely. "No, I think it came out perfectly. The world *doesn't* revolve around me, and it's amazing how excited I am to finally figure that out." He reached across the table and placed his fingers over hers, gently tracing circles across her knuckles as he spoke. "Thank you, Maribeth."

"I didn't do anything," she said.

"You've opened my eyes to the things that are important, and now I see why Dana loves it here. Everything is simpler, clearer." He took a sip of his coffee. "Less stressful."

"Would you," she started, and then wasn't sure whether it would be too forward to ask. But then again, she wanted to know, so she continued, "Would you want to live in Claremont?"

He'd started lifting the cup to his lips but paused halfway, his mouth sliding to the side as he thought about his answer. Then he shook his head. "At first I couldn't imagine living in a place this small, this rural. But over the past few weeks, I've come to love it here," he said.

"That's great," she said, but he lifted his hand as if he had more to say.

"However, I still have a company to run, and as much as Dana has tried to convince me it can be done long-distance, that just isn't the case. My board has managed okay while I've been gone, but they're holding what they can until I'm back and we can have a face-to-face." He shrugged. "Some things simply can't be handled with video conference or email, even in today's world."

Her hopes dropped a little, but she wasn't giving up yet. Obviously God had put Ryan in her life for a reason. And He'd put her in Ryan's life for a reason, too. She suspected that reason was to get him to church tonight, when Brother Henry had delivered a message that he'd undoubtedly needed to hear. But did God plan on Ryan staying in her life?

Please, God.

"Do you want another one?" he asked.

At some point in all of her thought process, she'd drained her cup. "Oh, no," she said. "I'd never sleep tonight." Which was laughable, because she suspected she wouldn't sleep anyway; her newly recognized feelings for Ryan would surely keep her awake, or perhaps dreaming of how things might have been. Might still be?

But how would it work? With him in Chicago and her in Claremont?

"Okay then, how about a walk across the square?" he asked.

She thought about the brace on his leg, and the fact that she had almost stopped noticing his slight limp. In fact, only when it'd taken him extra time to get around the car to try and open her door did she even think about it. But now she wondered how all of this walking tonight would affect his leg. Chances were he wouldn't say anything if it hurt him; that was the kind of guy Ryan Brooks had turned out to be. And she loved that about him. "Why don't we cut across the center so we can go by the fountain?" She didn't want to see the fountain as much as she wanted to limit the distance he'd have to walk on her account.

"Sounds like a plan." He left the waitress a generous tip, then placed his hand at the small of Maribeth's back as they left the Grind and started the short walk toward the fountain.

She noticed Ryan taking in the scene and wondered what it looked like to a city boy. She was accustomed to Claremont at night, the tiny yellow lights that showcased the architecture on the store eaves, the spotlights illuminating the fountain and the filigree shadows that the towering oaks cast across the grass. If Ryan had traveled as much as she suspected, this probably wasn't as incredible to him as it was to Maribeth.

"This is breathtaking," he said. "I had no idea on all of those visits when I rushed in and out of town that I was missing all of this."

Maribeth could hear the sincerity in his tone, and it warmed her heart. "I know. The first time I came to Claremont, met the people, saw the town, I knew I wouldn't leave."

A brief silence sat between them, the truth of her statement hitting her hard. She didn't want to leave. She'd had big city, bright lights and everything that went with it. Including all of the pain. She didn't want that again. And he'd said he couldn't live away from Chicago.

He put his arm around her and started walking away

from the fountain and toward her store. "You've done an amazing job, making your home here and building a successful business on your own. It's very similar, if you think about it, to what my father did. He was born in Jackson, Mississippi. Grew up on a cotton farm. I don't know if you knew that or not."

"Lawrence Brooks?" she questioned. She'd seen photographs and had heard plenty about the real estate magnate who'd single-handedly built his fortune.

He nodded. "Moved to Chicago and never went anywhere but up, or that's what he told Dana and me." He pointed to the Consigning Women sign backlit above her door. "A lot like you, leaving your life, your family and all behind to move to a town where you didn't know anyone, and starting a business that has undeniably impressed a certain CEO of a *Fortune* 500 company."

"You still want to make it bigger—add more stores, more notoriety, don't you?" she asked.

"I hate to see something so unique be contained to one place," he said, and when she looked up, she found that he was no longer looking at the store, but at her. "There's more to your saying no to my investing in your business than the fact that you are content where you are. You're afraid of something, Maribeth, and I honestly don't think it's failure. Success is written all over you, in everything you do, from the way you set up this store to the ensembles you create to the clothing you personally wear. You radiate success. So that isn't it, but something else scares you. And one day, I want you to trust me enough to tell me what it is."

Maribeth was shocked that after so little time together he already knew her so well, could see through her so well. She was afraid, so very afraid, of being exposed. Of her past coming back to haunt her, ruining her. "I do want to tell you," she said, "I want to…"

"But you're not ready yet," he completed.

"I'm not sure," she whispered, and her tears dripped free.

"It's okay," he said, tenderly brushing her tears away with his thumbs, then cradling her face in his palms. "I mean it, Maribeth. It is okay. I care about you, and I want to give you whatever time it takes to trust me. But I want you to stop holding yourself back." He brushed a soft kiss across her lips.

"Holding myself back?"

"I still think you should let me help you make this, your dream, reach its full potential. We could do it without losing ourselves to it the way my father did, Maribeth, because you aren't like him. You won't be relying on yourself alone. You'll have me, but, like I learned tonight, more importantly, you'll have God on your side. And you said you want to make a difference, that you're doing that by helping Nadia. But have you thought that if you increase your profits, you could actually donate more to her ministry?"

His words were exactly what she needed to hear. She didn't want to wait any longer. She needed to tell him the truth of her past, right now. "Ryan, I do want you to know," she started, but stopped when his phone started ringing in his pocket.

Ryan was enjoying every minute of his time with Maribeth, and it was too important to be interrupted. He silenced the phone and started to turn it off completely, but before he could, it rang again.

He growled, and she giggled. "I'll get rid of them quickly," he promised. Then he withdrew the annoying thing, glanced at the display showing his sister's name and answered. "Dana, what is it?"

"Ryan, I'm glad I got you. I kept trying, and I was afraid that you didn't have a signal, but something happened…." Her voice hitched, and she didn't finish the sentence.

He knew her well enough to know the tone. The last time she'd called him and sounded like this had been the day their father died. "Dana? What is it? What's wrong? Are you okay? Is the baby okay?"

"It isn't me. It's Oliver James."

"What about Oliver?" Ryan asked.

"When I got home, there were several messages on the machine. All of them were from Oliver, and he sounded urgent. He said he was trying to reach you and that it was vital that he get in touch with you tonight. He said he couldn't reach you on your cell."

Ryan thought of all the calls and texts that had come in while he'd been at the church, the ones he'd ignored. "Did he say why he needed me?"

"Only that there was a potential company crisis, and he thought you should probably get to Chicago as soon as possible to prepare a strategy."

"A company crisis," Ryan repeated, unable to comprehend what could've happened between the time he last spoke to Oliver, at about four this afternoon, and tonight. "I'll call him right now and handle it," he said.

"You…can't."

"Why not?"

"I called the number he left, his cell, to let him know I would try to get in touch with you and to see if there was anything I could do to help. His wife answered, and she was crying." She paused. "Oliver had a heart attack, Ryan."

"Is he…" He let the words hang. Oliver James was not only a respected board member for Brooks International, he was a friend. They worked together, golfed together. The thought of Oliver having a heart attack didn't compute. "Is he dead, Dana?"

"No, but she said it doesn't look good. They don't expect him to make it, Ryan. He's in the surgical intensive care unit at Northwestern Memorial." She paused. "He sounded stressed in his message. Do you think whatever was wrong caused this?"

"I don't know," he said, wishing he'd at least looked at the messages that he'd received during church. "But something is going on, and I should be there."

"I agree. I'll start getting your things together."

Ryan disconnected and looked at Maribeth, who'd taken hold of his free hand during the call and squeezed it gently now.

"You have to go?" she asked.

"One of my board members," he said, still not believing Oliver was in a hospital fighting for his life. "I just talked to him a few hours ago, and he's had a heart attack. They don't know if he's going to make it." He looked back at his phone, then glanced at the list of texts and missed calls. All from Oliver. "Something was wrong, and he was trying to reach me." He scanned each message, but all Oliver had mentioned was a crisis that had to be handled quickly. "A crisis," he said.

"Does that happen often?"

"It's business. Things happen all the time that might

be considered difficult, but Oliver has never been fazed, and I've never heard him call anything a crisis. I can't imagine what went wrong." He couldn't waste any more time. "I've got to get back to Chicago."

Chapter Eleven

Ryan was impressed with how quickly his pilot got the plane to Stockville and had Ryan back in Chicago and ready to deal with whatever crisis awaited. It didn't take him long to find out. Oliver had contacted every board member yesterday afternoon asking them to convene this morning and saying he was doing his best to make sure Ryan would be in attendance. According to Oliver, the matter could not be mentioned or handled via phone or email. Information would be waiting for them in the boardroom.

By the time Ryan arrived at Brooks International's corporate headquarters at 9:18 Thursday morning, the boardroom was filled, and each member sat delving through a stack of papers that began with a single white page stamped CONFIDENTIAL in red across the top.

The room was abuzz when Ryan entered, and each person uncharacteristically began trying to talk to Ryan first.

"We've got to handle this promptly, before this hits the news," one said.

"The loss to the company will be substantial but

won't ruin us. The public impression of Brooks International is what's at stake here—that's what we need to concern ourselves with."

Several others chimed in, and Ryan still had no indication what had initiated the semipanic, but he knew what should be their first priority. "Do we have any word on Oliver's condition?"

Jeffrey Frye, one of the oldest board members and one of Lawrence Brooks's most trusted advisers, looked at Ryan as though he had gone senile. "He's had a heart attack, Ryan. And I can guarantee you, this is what caused it." He lifted the stack of papers in front of him. "Now we need to deal with this before the press releases this story so the rest of us don't end up over there with our own rooms in the ICU."

Ryan took his seat at the head of the table and used that new concept of prayer, sending up a quick request for the right words. Because Jeffrey had watched Ryan grow up and was undeniably skeptical of Ryan's ability to effectively run the company after his father's death, he occasionally overstepped his bounds with his frankness. But he'd never insulted Ryan at the board table. "Jeffrey, I understand that you are concerned about this crisis. And I haven't had the opportunity to review the information, but I will momentarily, and I can promise you it will be handled promptly and efficiently. But first, I want to know if there has been any change in Oliver's condition."

"No change, sir," Angela Redding, the company's chief financial officer, said, her face drawn and eyes bloodshot, probably the same way Ryan's were, since he hadn't slept, either. Angela and Oliver were close;

their families were friends and often vacationed together.

"We all need to pray that changes soon," Ryan said, and Angela's obvious surprise at his words was mirrored on the faces of every other person at the table. Prayer had never been mentioned at a Brooks board meeting before, but it had now, and it felt good bringing God on board, too.

"Yes, sir, we do need to pray," Angela said.

Ryan looked squarely at Jeffrey. "Now we'll handle this." He flipped over the top page and scanned the interoffice memo Oliver had created. It summarized yesterday afternoon's chain of events, which did, in fact, constitute a crisis.

Okay, God. I'm counting on You to see me through.

For the next two hours, the board discussed what Oliver had learned from one of his friends at the *Tribune*. The paper had been featuring a series of stories on the horrors of human trafficking over the past few weeks, and according to Oliver's friend, tomorrow's paper would announce that an exclusive resort in Thailand, owned by Brooks International, was in fact a front for the largest human trafficking organization in that country.

The next two pages outlined Ryan's donations to Nadia's ministry and stated that Oliver feared the donations would now be seen as a sign of guilt and awareness by Brooks International. However, from all indications, the Thai government had arrested the individuals responsible for the crimes yesterday afternoon and were now working hard to ensure the safety and well-being of all known victims.

Ryan was sickened at the thought of one of their

properties being used to conduct what was basically sex slavery. He'd been so appalled at the numbers Nadia had provided him regarding the situation in her birth country that he'd wanted to help, but he hadn't considered the possibility that one of his own investments was a part of the horrific problem.

Now he had to fix it.

Ryan had been with his father when he toured the potential property, a beach resort on the island of Ko Yao. Remote but still accessible, the place was surrounded by secluded beaches, rain forests and uninhabited islands. The hotel had twenty-eight luxury villas, designed in traditional Thai architectural style, each villa facing the beach with its own private garden.

It was one of the more valuable Brooks International properties. But Ryan, like everyone else seated at the table, now knew that its reputation would be marred. People would see the resort and think about what happened in it. Perhaps the seclusion that had appealed to Ryan's father wasn't such a great thing after all, because the children and young women who had been taken there had a harder time getting away.

Ryan's jaw clenched. How could this have happened? He thumbed through the report again. Not all of the hotel staff were implicated, but enough that the government was involved with the "substantial arrests." Oliver's memo said the story would hit the *Tribune* tomorrow, and naturally every news outlet would pick it up at breakneck speed. This was a Brooks property, after all. And Brooks properties were the best.

"We saw where you gave a personal donation to this Women's Lighthouse ministry," Jeffrey said, "merely last week. And then Oliver had that ministry on the list of projects to fund this week, and we approved it. What made you donate that money? And what on earth had Oliver recommending it to us when something like this was going on there?"

Patience. Ryan would need patience to deal with Jeffrey Frye today. He thought of Maribeth. When he'd left her last night, she'd hugged him and told him she would be praying that everything went okay. He was almost certain he could feel the results of her prayers now. Because instead of losing his temper toward his father's old friend, he said, "I learned about the human trafficking problem in Thailand last week from the young lady who started the Women's Lighthouse ministry after visiting a church her grandfather supports in Thailand. Her cause was so compelling and the problem so horrific that I felt led to help, and I did." He noticed Angela was nodding, as were several others. But the majority still looked shell-shocked that they had ended up in this predicament at all.

Milton Morris, head of marketing, cleared his throat. "Mr. Brooks, I believe the best way to handle this is with the truth, and then with something positive in the public eye."

Finally. Someone bringing a helpful idea to the table. "Go ahead, Milton," Ryan said.

"We beat the media to the punch. You issue a statement that you had no knowledge of illegal activities taking place in any of the Brooks properties until today, that those who were responsible have been arrested and that you find human trafficking detestable."

"And what about the donation and the pledged contributions toward the Women's Lighthouse?" Jeffrey asked.

"Again, the truth. That you learned about the organization last week, saw it as a worthy cause and wanted to help the victims and prevent future victims."

"That's fine for putting a bandage on the problem," Jeffrey continued. "But it does nothing for the fact that the company's image will be scarred permanently after this gets out."

Milton leaned forward in his seat and placed his hands on the papers in front of him. "That's why I said we need to also add something positive, and I personally think if you could make it tie in to the problem in Thailand, in the same way that Ryan's donation to the Women's Lighthouse ties in, then that will show—"

"Guilt," Jeffrey completed.

"I don't think so," Milton continued. "I believe it will show we agree that it's a terrible tragedy and that we want to be involved with helping those suffering from it in any way."

Jeffrey shook his head, but Angela said, "I agree."

The conference intercom buzzed. Ryan knew they wouldn't be bothered except for an emergency, so he pressed the button and said, "What is it?"

Marie, his assistant, spoke quickly. "Mr. Brooks, the *Chicago Tribune* is calling for a statement. They are on line one. And CNN is on line two."

Ryan could hear more buzzing as she spoke that probably indicated additional phone lines held various other news media from around the country. "Tell them all that I will give them a statement in a half hour," he said, needing to confer with his board on exactly what to say.

"Yes, sir," she said, then the intercom disconnected.

"Okay, I want to hear our best options." He looked to

Milton. "And since I'd typically rely on our public responsibilities board member for help, I'm going to need to switch gears this time. Milton, I believe a marketing perspective is the best approach. What do you think?"

Milton nodded at Angela, then looked to Ryan. "From a marketing standpoint, it'd be good to not only show that you are helping with the problem in Thailand, but introduce something new. Take the focus off of that resort, if possible."

"Any ideas on how to do that?" Ryan asked.

"We don't have any acquisitions that haven't already been announced," Robert Taylor, head of acquisitions, stated.

"We could increase our donations to the Women's Lighthouse," Angela offered.

"That doesn't involve more than writing a check, and we'll be accused of simply trying to buy our way out of the negative association with human trafficking," Milton said. "Perhaps a way to incorporate support and recognition of the Women's Lighthouse in a way that draws attention to the ongoing problem…and our continuing stance on correcting it."

"I've got it," Ryan said. He proceeded to tell the board what he had in mind…and then said another prayer that Maribeth would agree.

Chapter Twelve

Maribeth had spent the majority of the day on the highest part of Lookout Mountain, where, naturally, she had no cell service whatsoever. Thursday's schedule called for the campers to take on the longest and most elevated trail on the mountain, and it lasted the entire day. She'd prayed for Ryan continually and that whatever he faced in Chicago wouldn't be too difficult. She also prayed for his friend Oliver and hoped to hear good news from Ryan about his recovery.

When he left last night, he'd promised he'd call today and that he'd come back to Claremont as soon as he could. He said he'd miss her, and she believed him.

But he'd also said he couldn't live here, so any return would be temporary. That truth had haunted her throughout the day, and she'd had to concentrate to keep her mind focused on the camp, on leading the Bible studies and on guiding the teens through the trails.

But the entire time, she kept asking herself the same questions. If she loved Ryan—and she believed she did—would she be willing to move to Chicago to be with him? Could she handle living in a large city? And what would happen to Consigning Women? If she allowed Ryan to make it bigger, as he said, then wouldn't that draw more attention to her, and wouldn't her past come out? Who was she kidding? If she and Ryan were to start dating, the media would dig up her past and reveal that she was *that* girl from seven years ago.

And regarding that, when should she tell Ryan about her famous ex?

So many questions. So few answers.

By the time she returned to the barn at the end of the camp day, it was nearly four-thirty in the afternoon. She'd left her phone in the barn because she'd known it would be useless where they traveled today, and she quickly grabbed it to see if Ryan had called. He had, three times. And he'd sent a text, too.

I need to explain. Call me ASAP. I miss you.

She smiled, those last three words settling on her heart. He missed her. This would all work out somehow. She started to dial but stopped when Dana entered the barn.

"Maribeth," she said, "I'm so sorry. I know you told him not to do it, and I'm not sure why he did. I've been texting him and calling, but he won't answer my calls and only texted that he needs to talk to you first."

The first words of Ryan's text were suddenly the ones that stood out: *I need to explain.* "What did he do?"

"He announced that Brooks International had plans to fund a chain of consignment stores, Consigning Women, that would focus on providing celebrityworthy outfits to the public for a consignment price. Your concept, your store. He's taking your idea and profiting from it, and—" she shook her head "—that's like something Daddy would have done, back when he was so shrewd and calculating in business. I never thought Ryan would do anything like that, and I sure didn't think he'd do that to you."

Maribeth felt as though she'd been punched in the stomach. She sat on a nearby hay bale and wondered what had happened since last night. "Did he mention my name?" she asked.

"Yes, he gave you the credit for the concept, but still…he didn't have your permission, did he?"

"No," she whispered and then rubbed her temples with her fingers. Would people associate her with the nickname from way back then?

Dana sat beside her and enveloped her in her arms. "I'm so sorry."

"I worked so hard to just be…me." She shook her head. "Now it's going to start all over again."

"What?" Dana asked.

"You'll see." Maribeth's phone rang. She knew before looking that Ryan was on the other end. She answered, "Why?"

Dana mouthed, *I'm sorry,* then stood and walked out of the barn.

"Maribeth, I didn't want to hurt you. I just need to explain."

She took a deep breath, let it out. "Okay, explain."

"If you haven't seen or heard the news yet, we learned today that one of our resorts in Thailand has been used as a front for human trafficking."

"Wh-what?"

"It's true, and that's what Oliver James found out yesterday afternoon, just before his heart attack."

"Oh, Ryan," she said, suddenly forgetting her own troubles in light of his.

"And because of my donation to Nadia's charity, the media believed we knew about what was happening at the property and then gave the contribution as a sign of a guilty conscience."

"But…that's not true."

"I know, but they didn't. And that's why our board convened this morning to determine a way to salvage the reputation of Brooks International in the public eye when all of the news hit, which happened a few hours ago."

Her mind reeled from taking it all in, but she still didn't understand. "What does this have to do with you expanding Consigning Women? I didn't give you permission to do that."

"You said you'd think about it, so I thought—"

"I didn't give you permission," she interrupted. "I didn't." Yes, she'd been thinking about it, and even considering the possibility, but she'd been so afraid of what might come out—what would come out soon, if it hadn't already.

"Maribeth, the reason I told them about Consigning Women is because it's such a positive concept, providing something nice for those who typically wouldn't be able to afford it. And I also announced that a portion of every sale's profit will be donated to charity, specifically the Women's Lighthouse."

She liked that idea, really. But she wasn't ready to be thrust in the limelight again, and she had a feeling with his announcement she'd be put there, front and center.

And she'd done such a good job of hiding in Claremont. "I didn't want you to do it," she said simply, not wanting to explain why. Last night she'd almost told him about her past. If she had, would he have done this?

But she didn't have to worry about telling him now. He'd find out soon enough anyway. The media would probably have a field day at her expense again.

"We can do this together," he said. "I want to be with you, Maribeth, and this business will be a way to make that happen."

So he wanted to be with her in business. What about in life? And in love? And what about the fact that he'd given her idea to the world? "Ryan, I can't trust you anymore." She disconnected, powered down her phone and walked to her car.

Chapter Thirteen

"I've been trying to reach her all afternoon, Dana. She won't take my calls," Ryan said Friday evening. "I've got to tell you, I wouldn't have done it if I'd realized how much it would upset her. I honestly thought she'd see the good that could be done from expanding her business. Wednesday night, before I left, she was about to tell me something. The more I thought about it, the more I believed she was going to tell me we could do this together, expand Consigning Women and work together to help others in a big way."

"She never told you to do it," Dana said. "And you have no way of knowing whether she would've told you that on Wednesday or not. You shouldn't have guessed about something so important, Ryan."

"Dana, the media jumped on coverage of this human trafficking ring so quickly that we didn't have a lot of time to determine a combative strategy for the firestorm. Announcing the positive aspect of Maribeth's idea not only helped Brooks International with the situation now but also allowed for the ability to help so many more people and raise awareness for Nadia's ministry. This is so much more than writing a check. The board members conferred and decided that we needed to do something more permanent, something that didn't appear as though we were merely trying to fix the problem with cash. And think of the publicity this is already garnering for Maribeth's upcoming stores. She's said she wanted to make a name for herself, and she's also said she was considering going bigger." He shifted the phone to his other ear while he watched yet another news broadcast about Brooks International.

"Considering isn't the same thing as authorizing," Dana said. "I honestly believe she doesn't want any more stores."

"But this is such a positive thing, the ability to make a difference the way she wanted, donating a portion of profits to the Women's Lighthouse."

"For some reason, Maribeth doesn't see it that way," Dana said. "She was so distraught at the camp today that she had to leave early."

Ryan hated that he'd upset Maribeth, and all he wanted to do was go back to Claremont and hold her, but he'd agreed to an interview on CNN for their broadcast tonight, so he'd had to head to Atlanta first. "I've got the CNN interview, but then I'm coming to see Maribeth and work this out." If she was so against the store expansion that it would cost him their relationship—which had barely even gotten started—then he'd do away with the idea. She was more important, and he'd just donate to the Women's Lighthouse on his own and let the media accuse him of trying to buy his way out of a problem.

But Ryan couldn't help but wonder what was holding her back. Maribeth was the type of person who cared about others and went out of her way to have an impact on their lives. The fact that she volunteered an entire month of her summer to the church camp proved that fact, helping every morning with the kids until she went straight to her store to round out a workday of nearly twelve hours. A person who would do that would want to take every opportunity to help those in need. But she didn't want to take this one. Why?

He sat in the greenroom preparing for his interview and watching a wall filled with current newscasts on the display monitors. One of the screens, which a moment ago had shown the Brooks International headquarters building, switched to a photo of a scantily clad woman climbing up pool steps, her dark hair slicked back and falling over the upper half of her body. And apparently that was all that was covering her beautiful flesh.

Maribeth.

"Dana, I've got to go," he said, and disconnected.

Ryan's heart clenched in his chest. The monitors were set to closed caption, and he scanned the details displayed across the bottom of the screen.

And in another bizarre twist of news involving Brooks International and CEO Ryan Brooks, we've learned that the woman behind the Consigning Women idea is none other than the girl the world met seven years ago as Sweet Marie, a nickname given to her by her boyfriend at the time, Jaxson Gregory. Now the attractive lady has snagged another rich man's attention.

Ryan gripped the chair and continued reading, every word hitting him like a sucker punch to the gut.

No stranger to gorgeous females, the Brooks CEO

previously dated Nannette Kelly Sharp, now the wife of Yankees third baseman Alex Sharp. A photo of Ryan and Nannette filled the left side of the screen, while a photo of Maribeth and Jaxson Gregory filled the right.

Anger rippled through Ryan, so much so that his vision blurred, and he could no longer make out the words crossing the screen.

Maribeth had dated Jaxson Gregory? He'd told her about Nannette. Why hadn't she told him about Jaxson?

And the broadcast missed the boat on one huge detail. Maribeth had done more than snag Ryan's attention over the past few weeks.

She had his heart.

And right now, his heart pounded so violently that his pulse hammered in both ears.

More photos of a scantily clad Maribeth covered the screen. Ryan turned off the monitor. He didn't need to see the screen to know that he'd been fooled again.

Chapter Fourteen

Merely two hours after he'd completed the interview at CNN, Ryan stood at the entrance of John and Dana's barn. He'd wasted no time leaving the CNN Center, and Ned had his plane ready to go as soon as Ryan reached the tarmac and a car waiting for him when they landed in Stockville. Everything was set for him to see Maribeth and tell her what he'd decided during that interview.

But Ryan wasn't ready to see her yet. He had to make sure he meant the words he'd said, and he knew who could help him decipher the truth behind the pain cloaking his heart.

He entered the tack room, grabbed a green apple and then took the treat to the other end of the barn and whistled toward the massive animal that set this entire thing in motion when he'd tossed Ryan to the ground.

Onyx exhaled through his nose, widened his eyes and arrogantly swished his tail.

"I need to go somewhere, and I want you to take me," Ryan said. "And in case you're wondering, I won't take no for an answer."

The stallion's head lowered, and he huffed out another breath. Then he slowly walked toward Ryan.

Ryan held his palm steady as Onyx grew closer, until his velvety lips found the treat and snatched the apple from Ryan's hand.

Cautiously, Ryan saddled the horse, while Onyx tossed him an occasional irritated stare. But he allowed Ryan to get him ready, and when Ryan hissed at the pain of mounting the horse with his injured leg, Onyx stopped moving completely, as though trying to help his rider out.

"I appreciate that, buddy," Ryan said, running his hand down the stallion's powerfully muscled neck. "Now, take me where I need to go." He tapped his good leg against the horse's side and Onyx surged forward without hesitation.

Minutes later, Ryan found himself at the base of Jasper Falls, the exact place he'd first kissed Maribeth... and the first time he'd thought he felt a hint of God in his world. "Whoa," he said to Onyx, and the horse stopped and waited.

While Ryan closed his eyes and prayed.

"God, I have no doubt You've been behind this whole thing. The accident that caused me to connect with Maribeth. Her business idea that kept me in Claremont. Even the church and the town that I've gained a fondness for—and a respect for—over the past few weeks. You know what I feel for Maribeth, and You know how much all of this stuff is killing me inside. The Jaxson Gregory mess. Those pictures." His throat clenched at the memory of the photographs that marred Maribeth's beauty, made her something for guys to lust after rather than treasure.

"God, You know how angry I was at her for not telling me about him, about why she didn't want to share her idea. But now I realize…that I brought her biggest fear to light. And then *I* was mad at *her*. Those photos might never have resurfaced if it wasn't for me, Lord." The truth of that statement stabbed his heart. He had no doubt that when they'd gotten interrupted by Dana's call about Oliver on Wednesday, she'd been close to telling him the truth.

"She would have told me, wouldn't she, God? I just didn't wait. I didn't give her a chance. And because of that, her fear is a reality." The memory of those pictures flared, and he pushed it away. "Forgive me, God, for not asking for Your guidance sooner. Maybe I wouldn't be in this mess if I had. And Lord, if it be Your will, help Maribeth forgive me, too."

He opened his eyes and felt the dampness of tears on both cheeks. Ryan couldn't remember the last time he cried, if ever. Lawrence Brooks saw tears as a sign of weakness, and Ryan had always agreed. Until now. Now he wiped them away knowing that they weren't a sign of weakness, but of strength. The strength to realize that he'd made a mistake and that he needed God to help him make things right.

When he returned to the barn, he found Dana waiting.

"I can't believe you rode him again," she said, walking up to meet them near the stalls. "We got home as you were riding away from the barn. I figured if you didn't return in an hour, we'd go see where Onyx dropped you this time."

"Thanks for the vote of confidence." Ryan climbed

out of the saddle and fought a wince when his left leg hit the ground.

"Ryan," she said, then frowned.

"Yeah?"

She glanced up toward the loft, blinked a couple of times and then said, "I'll help you with Onyx."

He knew that wasn't what she wanted to say, but he'd give her a moment to get her thoughts together before they talked about what was obviously on both of their minds. Maribeth.

Within minutes, they'd removed the saddle, blanket and bridle and then started brushing the horse down. Onyx remained still for the entire process, a different animal entirely than the wild stallion Ryan had encountered merely a few weeks ago. But then again, Ryan had changed plenty, too.

Dana brushed Onyx, but occasionally stopped to peer at Ryan's face. Finally, she asked, "Have you been crying?" Her voice was filled with a hint of concern… and a whole lot of shock.

"And praying," he said.

To his surprise, she didn't smile, but instead moved a hand to her mouth and allowed a few tears of her own to slip free. "Oh, Ryan."

"I hurt her," he said. "And I need to fix that. I just had to fix things with God first."

Dana nodded. "Well, it sounds like you've got your priorities in the right order. So what exactly are you going to do?"

"You'll see," he said. In fact, the whole world would see in about an hour. And, if God answered Ryan's prayer with a yes, Maribeth Walton would not only see, but believe.

* * *

As the nine o'clock news aired, Maribeth watched the television in horror as photo after photo of her posing provocatively filled the screen. The entertainment news programs had been showing them repeatedly for the past several hours, beginning with *OK! TV,* then *Inside Edition* and *Extra.* And now, she was the lead story on *Entertainment Tonight.*

"These pictures are just for me," he'd said. "No one else, I promise." And she'd believed him then, just as she'd believed him every other time. She wondered if Ryan was watching this now, or her family, or her friends—her church—in Claremont.

She didn't know how she'd start over again.

Tears falling, she turned up the volume to see how the media would spin it this time and caught the last two words of the current sentence.

"…Sweet Marie."

Maribeth's body trembled uncontrollably. She hated that name. Hated it.

"You may recall Jaxson Gregory, now one of Hollywood's most prominent leading men, started his career in music, but never had nearly the success in that field as he's had on the silver screen. However, he did have his one-hit wonder, the song that will never die and propelled him to the top of the music charts, as well as to the eyes of every Hollywood producer. 'Sweet Marie.' The shocking lyrics and accompanying photos that the man distributed of the 'innocent young thing he met at the beach' were star quality and undeniably sealed his fate as a heartthrob for—let's face it—every female in America. Everyone wanted to be Jaxson Gregory's 'Sweet Marie,' and while he's had a string of Hollywood beauties at his side ever since, it all began with the girl who wasn't Hollywood at all. But, I think you'd all agree, she has star quality, too."

Maribeth saw herself blowing a kiss to the camera, and then the newscaster was again on the screen.

"Apparently, Sweet Marie has grown up now. She's twenty-six years old and is going by her given name, Maribeth Walton. She lives in a small north Alabama town and runs a quaint boutique called Consigning Women, which Ryan Brooks happened to visit over the past month. And then, well, it seems Mr. Brooks must have been smitten with Sweet Marie, too, because now he's also trying to make the girl a star by bringing her tiny business to a whole new level and propelling the again unknown beauty back into the spotlight."

Angry at Ryan's betrayal, Maribeth muted the television.

No. She shook her head. She'd been so angry at him for sharing her idea, had honestly believed she couldn't trust him again. But this had nothing to do with trusting Ryan and everything to do with the fact that she'd been trying to hide the truth of her past. All of this could have been avoided if she'd told him the truth.

More photos, some Maribeth couldn't even recall taking, flashed across the screen like an elaborate scrapbook of her past, except this one didn't hold any memories she wanted to keep.

Her stomach pitched. Everything the news journalist said was true, and she deserved what she got for those horrible mistakes. She'd turned her back on her family, turned her back on God, and unfortunately, the evidence was there for the world to see. For the world to remember.

How would she leave her apartment again? Face all of the sweet, friendly people of Claremont again, when they'd undoubtedly seen the very worst in her?

God, tell me, why is this happening now? Why?

Her phone started ringing. She glanced at the display. Dana. Maribeth had ignored her friend's calls ever since the story first aired. But there was no reason to ignore them anymore. She might as well hear Dana's shock and disappointment now and get it over with.

She answered, "Dana, I'm so sorry. And embarrassed. I know you are ashamed—"

"That's enough." Dana's harsh tone wasn't what Maribeth expected, and she swiped through the tears that hadn't stopped falling.

"What?"

"I said that's enough. Your pity party is over, and you're going to pick yourself up, realize that God forgave you a long time ago and that that isn't the girl you are now, and you're going to keep living in Claremont with me and with everyone who loves you."

"I can't—I can't even think about showing my face in town. And Ryan—I can only imagine what he's thinking. I almost told him Wednesday night, but I didn't. And then I was so mad at him for bringing the business into the spotlight, because I knew what would happen, that the sins of my past would come out. But that isn't his fault. It's mine."

"Maribeth, I want you to do something, and I don't want you to ask me any more questions about it. Just do it."

"What is it?" she sniffed.

"Promise."

What else did she have to lose? "Okay. I promise."

"Go to your back door and let Ryan in."

"What? Dana?"

The click on the line let her know Dana was gone, and the hard knock from her kitchen let her know…she had a promise to keep. If she could. How in the world could she face him now? And how could she truly trust him again, after he'd ignored her request and shared her idea with the world?

She'd put on old flannel pajamas, even though it was seventy degrees, because they made her feel comfortable. Warm. Protected. Safe. She also had on her favorite worn slippers, the ones shaped like bunnies, the left missing an eye and the right missing a tail. Her hair hadn't been combed, and she'd been pushing it off her face ever since she'd started doubling over in tears. But she didn't stop to change her clothes, didn't dry her eyes, didn't comb her hair. He'd already seen her at her worst. She had no reason to impress him now. He'd never want her again.

"Maribeth, open the door." He wasn't yelling, but he wasn't speaking calmly, either—he was issuing an order. A few days ago, she'd have come back with a sassy reply and flirted with him while he waited for her to unlock the door. But that was when she felt fun and carefree. That was before he'd betrayed her trust. And before she felt like…damaged goods.

She unlocked the door and opened it.

Ryan had never wanted to see anyone so badly as he wanted to see Maribeth. Now, looking at her, her eyes swollen and tearstains down both cheeks, he'd never wanted to hold someone so badly, either. But those photos, and more than that, the words of the announcers, that she'd "snagged" another rich boy, kept him standing his ground.

Using every ounce of control he possessed, he said, "I've been thinking about it all afternoon, from when it first came out." His jaw clenched. "The whole Jaxson Gregory thing."

Maribeth closed her eyes. "I wish I could forget that name."

He could tell she was in pain, and he could only imagine what the firestorm that had started earlier today had done to her over the last few hours. He'd felt as if it'd taken a piece of him, and after seeing her now, he realized that it'd been much worse on Maribeth. "I'll admit that when I saw those photos and learned about everything, I was angry."

"I was angry, too," she said, "and hurt that you would do that to me, put me back in the spotlight when I'd worked so hard—" she sucked in a breath "—so hard to keep my past from coming back out. But then I realized that you didn't do it. I did."

The pain in her words, in her eyes, was almost more than he could take, because Ryan knew he'd caused it. "I realize now why you didn't want me sharing your idea, and I also realize that I hurt you."

Before he could say more, she said, "I shouldn't have done it, let him take those photos or had that kind of relationship with him back then. I was stupid, and I understand why you wouldn't want anything to do with me anymore," she said, her words shaky and trembling with emotion. "I really—I didn't think I'd see you again, and if you came back to hear me apologize, I will. I'm sorry. I should've told you about—"

He placed a finger against her mouth and shook his

head. "No, Maribeth. I don't want to hear an apology. That isn't why I'm here, not at all." The urge to hold her, to protect her, still burned through him, but he had to get his questions answered first. "I'm here because I have something to ask you, and I want you to promise me that when you answer me, you'll tell me the truth. I *need* to know that you'll tell me the truth, Maribeth."

She blinked, more tears fell and she bit her lip. "There's nothing to lie about. That's me. You've seen it, and the whole world has seen it. I'm the one who did—" she pointed toward the television in the next room "—all of that. I deserve this."

"No, you don't, Maribeth. That isn't who you are anymore. I know that, you know that and your friends and family know that, too. And if I'd understood why you wanted to keep yourself out of the public eye, I'd never have mentioned Consigning Women outside of Claremont. I was wrong."

Her dark eyes were swimming in tears when she looked up and seemed to finally understand what he was saying. "What?"

"Promise to tell me the truth. I have one question, and I want your honest answer, regardless of whether it hurts me." He paused. "Or you."

She rubbed the dampness from her cheeks. "Okay."

He took a deep breath, gathered his courage and asked what he most wanted to know. "Do you love me? Not my business or my status or my assets. But do you love *me?*"

"With every part of me, I love you," she answered, and Ryan had no doubt that she meant every word. He'd prayed to God to give him the strength to believe her and to see the truth of their relationship. And he did.

He saw it clearly now. She loved him, and she hadn't wanted to hurt him by allowing him to know the truth of her past. But she would've told him; Ryan knew that now. When she was ready, she would've told him.

"Maribeth," he said, "I don't know if you can, but I've been praying the whole way here that you will forgive me."

"Forgive you? It isn't your fault. I'm the one that did all of that," she said.

"You asked me not to expand your business. You didn't want attention brought to you, and I ignored your request. I now see how wrong I was, and I want you to forgive me."

"I do," she said.

Relief flooded through him as he took a small step into her tiny kitchen. He'd never been on this side of the consignment store, the back portion that served as her kitchen and living room, with a circular wrought iron staircase that presumably led to her upstairs rooms. Like the consignment shop, this area had style. The room decorated in reds and golds was classically fashionable, like the woman standing merely a foot away.

But she didn't look fashionable now, in her worn pajamas, pitiful slippers and uncombed hair. On the contrary, she looked…lovable. And he loved her, so much that when she was hurting, he hurt. Especially because he knew he'd caused her this pain.

"Let me hold you," he said, and to his dismay, she shook her head.

"No, Ryan."

"Because I caused all of this?" he asked, thinking he'd do anything to go back one day and never mention Consigning Women to the board or to the reporters.

"No, because you'll hold me, and I'll fall. Hard. The way I did back then. I love you. I've told you that, and I meant it. But being with you would put me right back where I was before. I've tried so hard to make it on my own, to be my own person, not Jaxson Gregory's ex-girlfriend, not the inspiration for 'Sweet Marie.' I want to be Maribeth Walton, the girl who loves God and loves clothes and loves Claremont. That's all I want to be."

"Can I show you something?" he asked.

She looked confused, as though he couldn't possibly have a reason to keep talking to her, but he did, and it was an important one. "Show me what?" she asked.

"Come here." He took her hand and was thankful that she didn't pull away, but allowed him to lead her toward the next room, her cozy living area, where the television sat in the center.

"I do not want to watch it again," she said, shaking her head.

He found the remote and turned the channel to CNN. "Just one more broadcast," he said.

"No, Ryan," she whispered, but then she sucked in her breath when the image on the screen…was Ryan.

He increased the volume and allowed her to hear.

"So what you're saying is you had no idea that Maribeth Walton was Jaxson Gregory's inspiration for his famed song when you met her, learned about her business and decided to invest in her business."

"I didn't, and I didn't need to know anything about it. That isn't who she is now," Ryan said, and when the journalist looked skeptical, Ryan's voice took on an assertive tone. "I'm sure if we all looked back seven years, or maybe twenty-seven years in your case, John, we'd all find something we'd rather not have replayed for public consumption."

The man smiled. "Agreed, but this isn't something most people have buried in their closet, wouldn't you agree?"

"No, some have things much worse," Ryan said, his tone almost…a warning.

The interviewer looked a little uncomfortable and shifted gears. "And it's coincidental that her business plans to donate a portion of profits to this—" he glanced at his reference sheet "—Women's Lighthouse ministry, which happens to assist victims of human trafficking and attempt to prevent the industry from growing in Thailand, the country where we learned this morning that Brooks International actually owns a resort that had been a front for that very industry."

"No, it isn't a coincidence. Maribeth had already started donating a portion of her profits from her original store to the organization. She was so convinced by their ministry that she wanted to support them as much as she could. With Brooks International assisting her in taking her business to the next level, she'll be able to take her donations to the next level, as well."

"Okay, Mr. Brooks, I can see you've got an answer for all of my questions. I have just one more for you."

"Fine. Go ahead," Ryan said.

Ryan squeezed Maribeth's hand. "In case you're wondering, I requested this question to be asked, and to get the interview, they granted the request."

Maribeth's eyes widened, and she stared at the small screen.

"This one is a little more…personal, but I suspect our viewing audience is eager to know the answer. How would you describe your relationship with Marie—excuse me, Maribeth Walton?" he asked, smiling.

Maribeth held her breath. "What are you going to say?" she whispered.

"Watch and see," he said simply, his words near her left ear sending a trickle of goose bumps down her arm.

"My relationship with Maribeth Walton," he said on the screen, "begins with my respect for her as a person. She's intriguing and fascinating. She has a stronger faith than anyone I've ever met, and I believe that faith was developed after she went through the difficult time and the ridicule that you've so flagrantly displayed today. She moved away from her home, started her life over and built a profitable business using an ingenious concept that was all her own."

"That's all well and good," the man said, "but it still doesn't tell me what I asked. What is your personal relationship to Maribeth Walton?"

"I love her, and nothing you or any other journalist has attempted to say about her today or show about her today will ever change that."

Applause sounded from the television as Ryan shook the man's hand and they concluded the interview.

Maribeth turned toward the man she'd totally fallen in love with. "You love me?"

"With every part of my being," he said, and then added, "I had to postpone the interview twice this afternoon because I couldn't wrap my head around it all. I was angry, and I thought I'd been fooled again, that you'd played me the way Nannette had."

"But I'd never—" she started, and again, he put a finger to her soft lips and smiled.

"I know. And I believe you. I trust you, Maribeth, and I always will." He ran a finger down her cheek. "And after that interview, I spent some time with God."

"You did?"

Ryan nodded. "I needed to get things right with Him, so I could get things right with you. I love you. I want a relationship with you, starting now and lasting forever."

"But you're in Chicago, and I'm here," she whispered as he pulled her close and kissed her.

"And we'll work that out," he said.

The applause from the television continued and continued and continued, but at some point, Ryan had turned off the TV.

"Oh, right," he said, grinning. "There's something else you need to see." He took her hand and led her through the living area and into the front of the store, where the applause grew louder.

Maribeth neared the windows displaying her newest ensembles and soon saw the source of the noise. Ryan opened the door and Maribeth glanced down. "Oh, Ryan, they can't see me like this."

"They'll see you the same way I do. Maribeth Walton. The friend they adore, and the woman I love."

He gently tugged her outside, where it appeared the entire town had gathered…and were clapping. They were applauding her past mistakes? Surely not. But then she noticed Nadia and Jasmine on the shoulders of Casey Cutter, Nadia's boyfriend, who must've come home from college today, and Cory Shields. A sign stretched between the girls read, Congratulations on

Your Growing Business! And in smaller letters beneath, Claremont Loves You!

Her tears were instant. "Oh, my," she said, her voice cracking with emotion. She scanned the crowd and saw all of the store owners from the square, Brother Henry and Mary, John and Dana, Landon and Georgiana and Abi, and what appeared to be the entire congregation from the Claremont Community Church. And then, to the side, she saw them: her family. "Dad? Mom?"

Her father, mother and both sisters were crying and smiling. "Ryan called us," her dad said, "and we got in the car and headed this way. We're proud of you, honey. You've come so far, and it looks like you're not done yet. We're excited about your business expanding, and we want you to know we support you a hundred percent."

"I—" she struggled to make her throat work "—I don't know what to say."

"Well, I know what I'd like to say." Ryan faced the crowd and announced, "We're glad you've all been so supportive of the first Consigning Women store, and we hope that you'll visit each and every store when it opens, because we've got big plans in mind, and we're going to make a difference together." He looked to Maribeth. "If that's what you want, of course. We'll grow our business…as we grow our love."

Maribeth's heart swelled. Growing her business and growing their love. "That's exactly what I want."

Epilogue

R yan had never really visualized himself getting married. A year ago, he'd probably have said it'd never happen, and he'd probably have added a few choice words to the promise. But he'd stopped using those words now. And he'd stopped making promises he couldn't keep. Because he'd met a woman who, quite simply, had changed his life. She'd given him faith and opened his eyes and heart to love.

He took in his surroundings and grinned. Yeah, if he'd ever pictured his wedding, it wouldn't have been anything like this, with the entire tiny town of Claremont sitting on quilt-covered hay bales and waiting to see the woman who'd stolen his heart marry him at the entrance to a big red barn. He nearly laughed at his Chicago group attempting to look all Western. They were wearing the clothes Maribeth had helped them select, but they still looked as out of place as Ryan had when he first came to visit his sister. Not anymore. He blended in here, felt at home here, which was good, since he and Maribeth had decided to split their time between Claremont and Chicago. He'd bought them a lovely antebellum home about a block from the square in Claremont, and they'd have his apartment in Chicago. Until kids came, and then he'd get something with more room.

Kids. The thought of having a little girl who looked like Maribeth made him happy. He couldn't wait. Thankfully, she'd said she was eager to get started, too. Dana's baby boy, Holden, was seven months old now. If he and Maribeth had a baby in, say, a year, the cousins would be close. Worked for him.

And speaking of working for him, his entire board filled the second and third rows. Well, most of the board. Oliver James stood beside Ryan as best man. He'd made a full recovery, and Ryan thanked God every day for healing his friend. John and Landon were his other two groomsmen.

Ryan scanned John and Dana's log cabin, where he knew his bride waited to make her appearance. He was so eager to start their lives together, so blessed by everything God had given him. And he felt blessed by everything his father had given him, too. Because Lawrence Brooks had taught him plenty, about hard work and building a business from the ground up and about what it took to bring your business to the top. But something else his father had taught him, even if it had taken Ryan a few years to figure it out, was that nothing was done on your own. Everyone needed help. Everyone needed God. He believed Dana now, that their father had found faith before he died, and Ryan was extremely glad for that.

Cory Shields and Casey Cutter helped usher folks to their seats—or rather, their bales. And after Cory seated Chad and Jessica Martin, he waved Casey on to go get the next couple, and he moved to the front to speak to the groom.

"Mr. Brooks," he said, attempting to whisper but loud enough that Oliver, John and Landon undoubtedly heard. "Thank you for the tuition money. I'm starting back to college in the fall thanks to you, and I'll do what you say. I'll call you the minute I graduate with a transcript full of As and ready for a job."

"I have no doubt you will," Ryan said.

Oliver tapped Ryan's shoulder. "You're doing good now," he said.

Ryan saw the cabin door open and his beautiful bride step out on the arm of her father. "I know, Oliver," Ryan said. "I know."

The crowd stood as Maribeth made her way to the lamplit barn. Ryan had admired many of Maribeth's ensembles over the past few months as they planned their business and the wedding, but the simple lace dress that she wore now outdid them all. Her shoulders were bare, her hair held back by a pearl-embellished veil. The lace brushed the ground as she walked and somehow gave the impression that she was floating…to him.

"Who gives this woman to marry this man?" Brother Henry asked.

"Her mother and I." Maribeth's father kissed her cheek, shook Ryan's hand and then placed Maribeth's hand in Ryan's. "Take good care of her, son," he said.

"Yes, sir. I will."

Ryan glanced at her dress. "Jennifer Aniston?" he whispered.

She giggled. "Guess again."

Brother Henry smirked, but stopped his initial dialogue about marriage to let them finish.

"Scarlet Johansson."

"Wrong."

Her bridesmaids—her sisters, Ava and Deidre, and Dana—all covered their mouths to keep from laughing out loud. The groomsmen chuckled without care.

"Excuse me, but I believe we have people counting on a wedding here," Brother Henry said, and this time, the entire crowd laughed.

"Okay," Ryan conceded, "who is it?"

"It's Maribeth Walton," his stunning bride said. "This one is only for me…and only for you."

"Perfect."

* * * * *

Dear Reader,

We have all done things in our past that we wish we could do over. That's the way Maribeth felt about the troubles from her past. Those hidden secrets kept her from trusting, kept her from loving. And once the bandage had been ripped off the old wound, she found the strength to work through the pain and heal…with Ryan by her side.

Ryan had problems from his past, too. Suffocating in his father's shadow, he struggled to find his way out. But the only way he could truly shine was to follow his own heart and do what he believed was right by supporting the Women's Lighthouse.

Even though Ryan did what was right, and even though Maribeth's past eventually came out, neither happened without difficulty. Like Maribeth's story to the campers, we all face life's storms, but with Christ on our side, we survive like that house on the rock.

May God be with you through your storms, and may you find comfort in the story of Maribeth and Ryan finding their way through the storm to find each other…and, more importantly, to find God.

I enjoy mixing facts and fiction in my novels, and you'll learn about some of the truths hidden within the story on my website, www.reneeandrews.com. If you have prayer requests, there's a place to let me know on my site. I'll lift your request up to the Lord in prayer. I love to hear from readers, so please write to me at renee@reneeandrews.com. Find me on Facebook at www.facebook.com/authorreneeandrews. And follow me on Twitter at www.twitter.com/reneeandrews.

Blessings in Christ,

Renee Andrews

Questions for Discussion

1. Maribeth moved away from her hometown and her family to hide from the mistakes she made with Jaxson Gregory. Have you ever tried to run from a mistake? What was the outcome?

2. Is there a Jaxson Gregory lurking in your past? Do you still see the person? Have you found the ability to forgive him or her?

3. Do you still live in the same town as your family, like the majority of the folks in Claremont? Or are you away from family? What are the advantages and disadvantages of both?

4. Maribeth found teaching the youth at the Claremont Community Church a salve for her soul. Why do you think helping teens was so important to Maribeth?

5. How do you think growing up without a mother affected Ryan? Do you think he would have behaved differently if his father had remarried?

6. What do you think of Dana and Ryan's relationship? Do you have similar relationships with your siblings? What do you do when, in your opinion, a sibling is headed down the wrong path spiritually? Is it harder or easier to talk to a sibling who is going the wrong way than to a friend or acquaintance?

7. What did you feel during the scene where Maribeth saw the photos from her past on television? Whom do you think she thought of first when she knew all of America was learning her secrets?

8. Brother Henry came to visit Ryan even before Ryan had ever entered the church. How do you think this impacted Ryan's willingness to visit that particular church?

9. There are places in Claremont (and in my hometown, too) where a cell signal isn't available. What, if anything, would be beneficial about going to a spot where you knew you couldn't be reached?

10. Ryan had no trouble forgiving Maribeth for keeping her secret. Neither did the town of Claremont. Do you find this is typically the case in real life, or do you believe people aren't as willing to forgive? And if they aren't, what Bible verses could you use to help them see Christ's feelings on the subject of forgiveness?

11. Maribeth was something of a mentor to Nadia and Jasmine. Ryan proved to be the same thing to Cory. Have you ever been the person to whom a teen could turn for guidance? Have you ever turned to someone for guidance?

12. How did you feel about the way Ryan handled Jasmine's infatuation? Do you believe most men would have reacted the same way? Why, or why not?

13. Nadia's ministry, the Women's Lighthouse, is actually modeled on a real ministry that my children supported through college. Do you support any ministries? Why or why not? And if you do, which ministries do you feel the strongest about and why?

14. How do you think Maribeth's parents felt when they saw her history with Jaxson brought back up in the news? How do you think the people who lived near them, went to church with them, would have reacted after seeing the story about their daughter?

15. List the similarities between Onyx the horse and Ryan. How many can you find?

REQUEST YOUR FREE BOOKS!

2 FREE INSPIRATIONAL NOVELS
PLUS 2
FREE
MYSTERY GIFTS

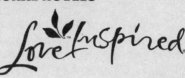

LI13R

SPECIAL EXCERPT FROM

Love Inspired

*Get ready for a Big Sky wedding...or fifty! Here's a
sneak peek at
HIS MONTANA BRIDE by Brenda Minton,
part of the **BIG SKY CENTENNIAL** miniseries:*

"Bad news," Cord said. "That was the wedding coordinator. She's quitting."

"Ouch. So now what?"

"I'm not sure."

"With no coordinator to help, will you call off the wedding?" Katie asked.

"No." There was too much at stake. The town needed this wedding and the money it would bring in. They had a bridge in need of repairs and a museum they couldn't finish without more funds. "I'll just figure out how to pull off a wedding for fifty couples, maybe get some media attention for Jasper Gulch and hopefully not mess up anyone's life."

"I think you'll do just fine. Remember, it's all about the dress."

"How long are you going to be in town, Katie?" He placed a hand on her back and guided her up the sidewalk.

"I'm not sure. I'm supposed to be helping my sister, but she seems to have escaped and left me here." She sighed and glanced at him.

"Do you think that as long as you're here..."

They were standing in front of the massive wooden doors that led to the church. She had a slightly red nose from the cool morning air and her lips were tinted with pink gloss. As long as she was there, she could be a friend. That wasn't

LIEXP0914

what he'd planned to say, but the thought framed itself as a question in his mind.

She was studying his face, waiting for him to finish.

"Maybe you could help me with this wedding?"

"I thought maybe you wanted me to run interference and keep the single women at bay. 'Hands off Cord Shaw,' that kind of thing." As she said it, somehow her palm came to rest on his shoulder as if they'd been friends forever.

It was the strangest and maybe one of the best feelings. It tangled him up and made him lose track of the reality that he was standing in front of the church. The door could open at any moment. And for the first time in years, a woman had made him feel at ease.

Can rancher Cord Shaw and Katie Archer pull off Jasper Gulch's latest centennial event without getting their hearts involved? Find out in HIS MONTANA BRIDE by Brenda Minton, available October 2014 from Love Inspired.

Danger and love go hand in hand in the small town
of Wrangler's Corner. Read on for a sneak preview of
THE LAWMAN RETURNS by Lynette Eason,
the first book in this exciting new series from
Love Inspired Suspense.

Sheriff's deputy Clay Starke wheeled to a stop in front of
the beat-up trailer. He heard the sharp crack, and the side
of the trailer spit metal.

A shooter.

The woman on the porch careened down the steps and
bolted toward him. Terror radiated from her. He shoved
open the door to the passenger side. "Get in!"

Breathless, she landed in the passenger seat and slammed
the door. Eyes wide, she lifted shaking hands to push her
blond hair out of her eyes.

Clay got on his radio and reported shots fired.

He cranked the car and started to back out of the drive.

"No! We can't leave!"

"What?" He stepped on the brake. "Lady, if someone's
shooting, I'm getting you out of here."

"But I think Jordan's in there, and I can't leave without
him."

"Jordan?"

"A boy I work with. He called me for help. I'm worried
he might be hurt."

Clay put the car back in Park. "Then stay down and let
me check it out."

"But if you get out, he might shoot you."

He waited. No more shots. "Stay put. I think he might be gone."

"Or waiting for one of us to get out of the car."

True. He could feel her gaze on him, studying him, dissecting him. He frowned. "What is it?"

"You."

He shot a glance behind them, then let his gaze rove the area until he'd gone in a full circle and was once again looking into her pretty face. "What about me?"

Red crept into her cheeks. "You look so much like Steven. Are you related?"

He stilled, focusing in on her. "I'm Clay Starke. You knew my brother?"

"Clay? I'm Sabrina Mayfield."

Oh, wow. Sabrina Mayfield. "Are you saying the kid in there knows something about Steven's death?"

"I don't know what he's doing here, but he called me and said he thought he knew who killed Steven and he needed me to come get him."

A tingle of shock raced through Clay. Finally. After weeks with nothing, this could be the break he'd been looking for. "Then I want to know what he knows."

Pick up THE LAWMAN RETURNS, available
October 2014 wherever
Love Inspired Suspense books are sold.

Hunter Jacobson wants no part of his grandfather's matchmaking. The lone cowboy is certain that's what the old man is doing when he trades part of their Montana ranch for Scarlett Murphy's shares of an old Alaska gold mine. Or is he running one of his legendary scams on the sweet single mom? A trip to Dry Creek, Alaska, reveals the truth—and brings Hunter and Scarlett face-to-face with a past family feud and a vulnerable present. But surprisingly it's the future that intrigues Hunter most…if he can get Scarlett to make him her groom.

❖ NORTH *to* DRY CREEK ❖

The road to Alaska is paved with love

Alaskan Sweethearts

by

Janet Tronstad

Available October 2014
wherever Love Inspired books
and ebooks are sold.

LI87914